W9-ATY-302

FEB 21

JUST BEYOND™

VOLUME 7:
THE PARENTS START
TO SUSPECT

Written by
R.L. Stine

Illustrated by
Kelly & Nichole Matthews

Lettered by
Mike Fiorentino

Cover by
Miguel Mercado

Just Beyond created by
R.L. Stine

Designer
Scott Newman

Assistant Editor
Michael Moccio

Associate Editor
Sophie Philips-Roberts

Editor
Bryce Carlson

ABDOBOOKS.COM

Reinforced library bound edition published in 2021 by Spotlight, a division of ABDO, PO Box 398166, Minneapolis, Minnesota 55439. Spotlight produces high-quality reinforced library bound editions for schools and libraries.
Published by agreement with KaBOOM!

Printed in the United States of America, North Mankato, Minnesota.
092020
012021

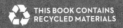

THIS BOOK CONTAINS RECYCLED MATERIALS

kaboom!™

BOOM! Studios, 5670 Wilshire Boulevard, Suite 400, Los Angeles, CA 90036-5679.

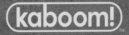

Library of Congress Control Number: 2020940843

Publisher's Cataloging-in-Publication Data

Names: Stine, R.L., author. | Matthews, Kelly; Matthews, Nichole, illustrators.
Title: The parents start to suspect / by R.L. Stine; illustrated by Kelly Matthews, and Nichole Matthews.
Description: Minneapolis, Minnesota : Spotlight, 2021. | Series: Just beyond; volume 7
Summary: Back at the Waldens' home, Zammy and Juniper struggle to control Parker and Annie while at the same time avoiding detection from the kids' parents, but the aliens forget about another family member who is following them.
Identifiers: ISBN 9781532147579 (lib. bdg.)
Subjects: LCSH: Camping--Juvenile fiction. | Families--Juvenile fiction. | Human-alien encounters--Juvenile fiction. | Parent and child--Juvenile fiction. | Adventure stories--Juvenile fiction. | Graphic Novels--Juvenile fiction. | Comic books, strips, etc.--Juvenile fiction.
Classification: DDC 741.5--dc23

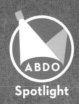

ABDO
Spotlight

A Division of ABDO
abdobooks.com

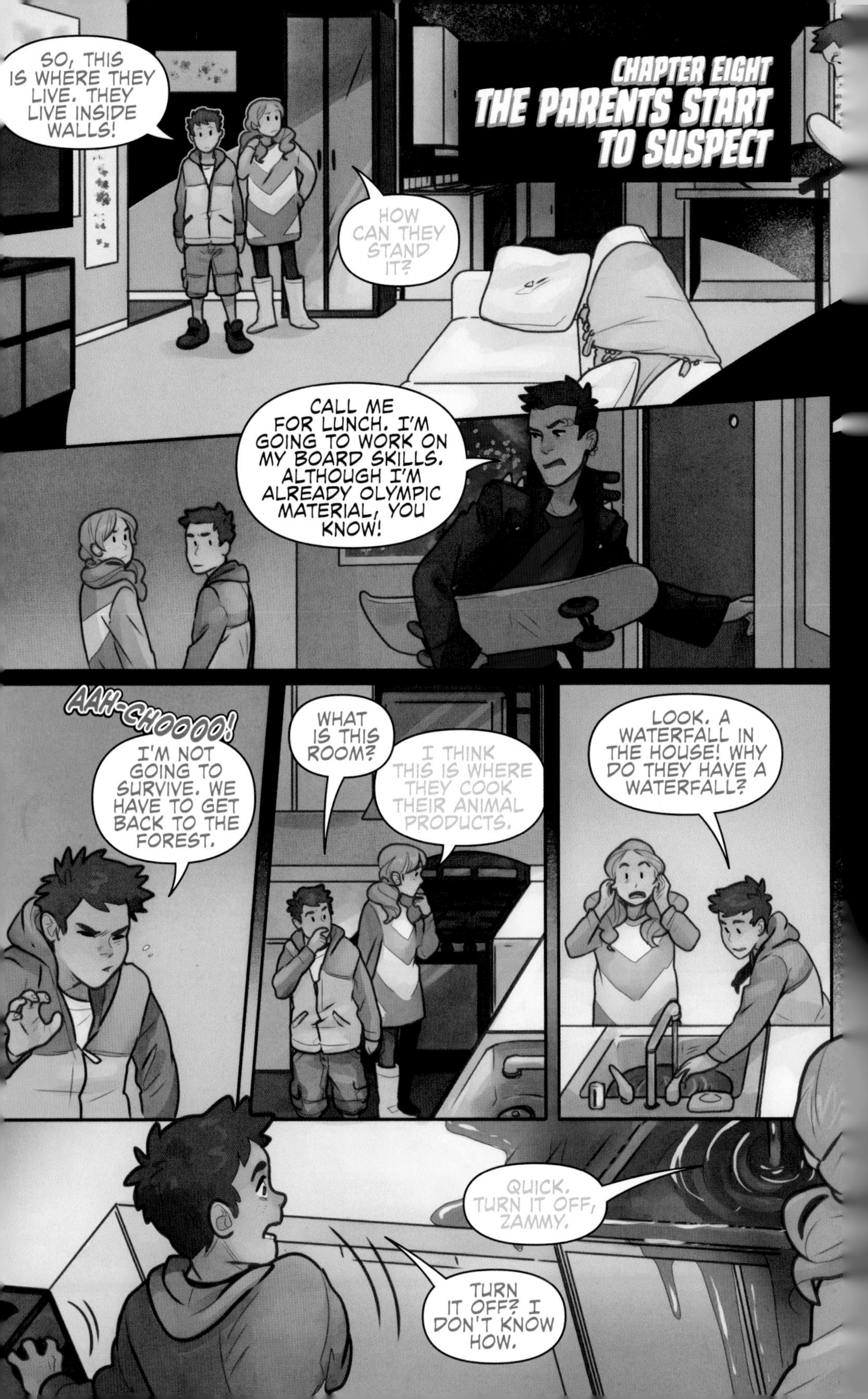
CHAPTER EIGHT
THE PARENTS START TO SUSPECT
SO, THIS IS WHERE THEY LIVE. THEY LIVE INSIDE WALLS!
HOW CAN THEY STAND IT?
CALL ME FOR LUNCH. I'M GOING TO WORK ON MY BOARD SKILLS. ALTHOUGH I'M ALREADY OLYMPIC MATERIAL, YOU KNOW!
AAH-CHOOOOO!
I'M NOT GOING TO SURVIVE. WE HAVE TO GET BACK TO THE FOREST.
WHAT IS THIS ROOM?
I THINK THIS IS WHERE THEY COOK THEIR ANIMAL PRODUCTS.
LOOK. A WATERFALL IN THE HOUSE! WHY DO THEY HAVE A WATERFALL?
QUICK. TURN IT OFF, ZAMMY.
TURN IT OFF? I DON'T KNOW HOW.

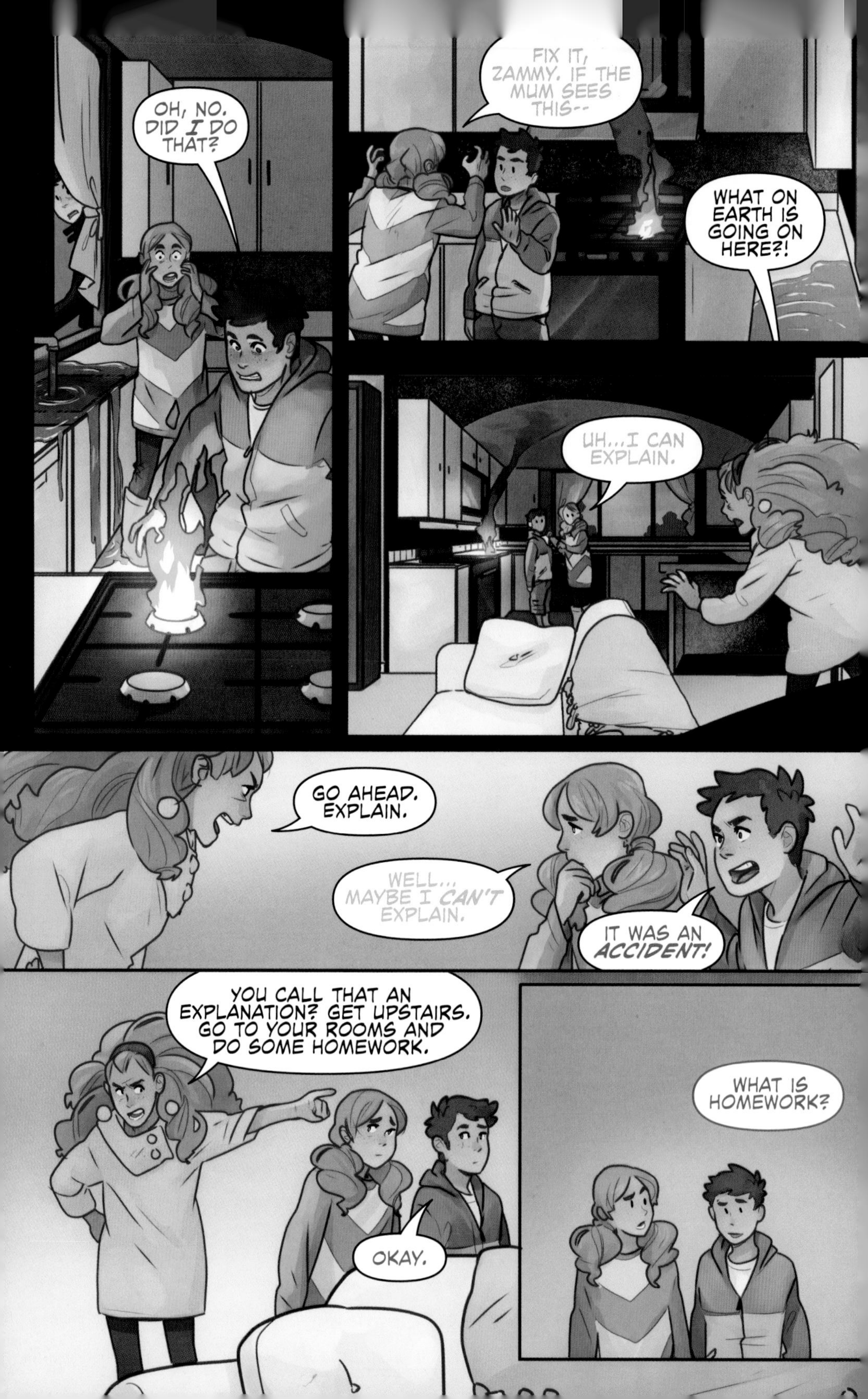
OH, NO. DID *I* DO THAT?
FIX IT, ZAMMY. IF THE MUM SEES THIS--
WHAT ON EARTH IS GOING ON HERE?!
UH...I CAN EXPLAIN.
GO AHEAD. EXPLAIN.
WELL... MAYBE I *CAN'T* EXPLAIN.
IT WAS AN *ACCIDENT!*
YOU CALL THAT AN EXPLANATION? GET UPSTAIRS. GO TO YOUR ROOMS AND DO SOME HOMEWORK.
OKAY.
WHAT IS HOMEWORK?

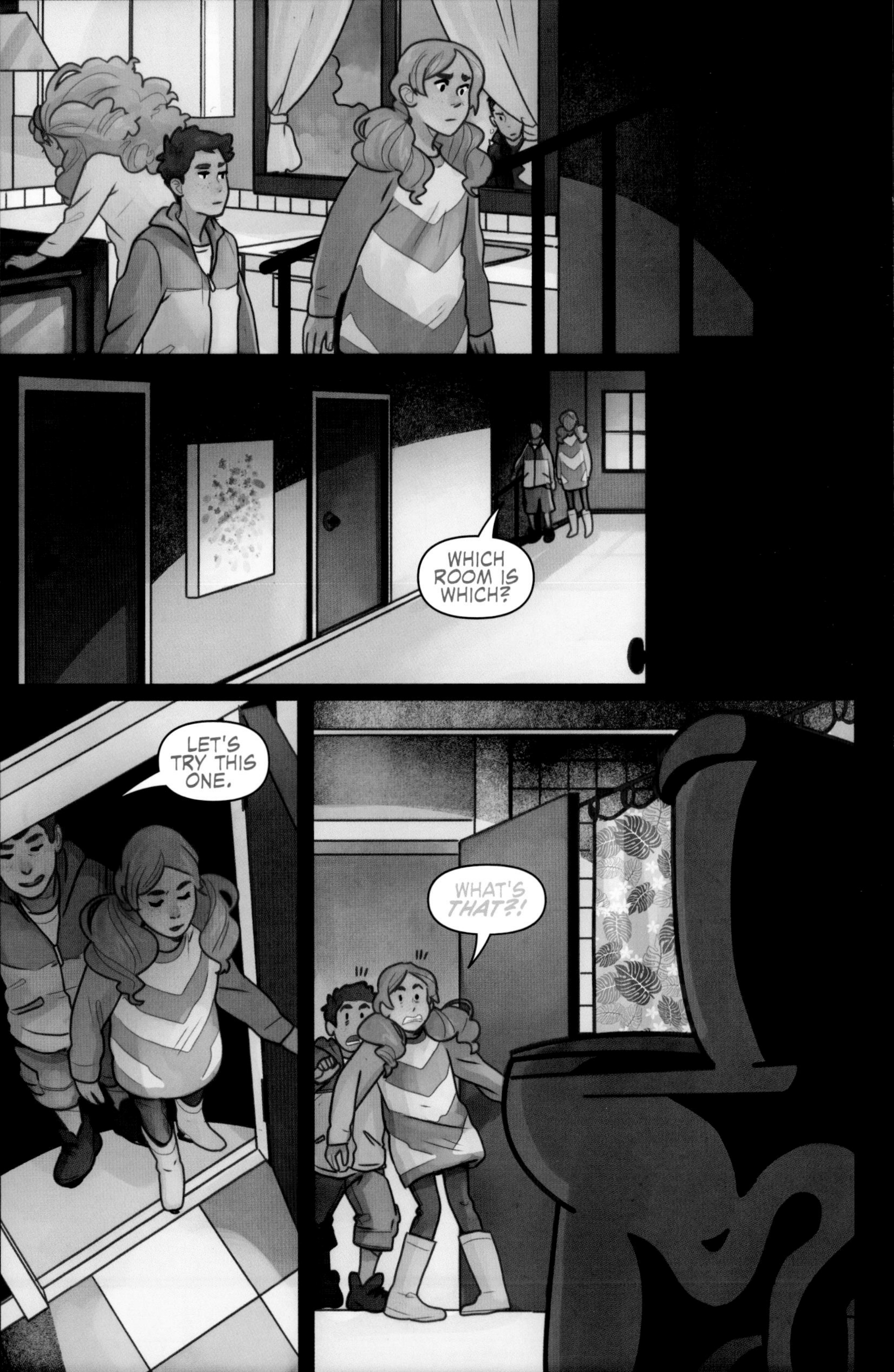
WHICH ROOM IS WHICH?
LET'S TRY THIS ONE.
WHAT'S *THAT?!*

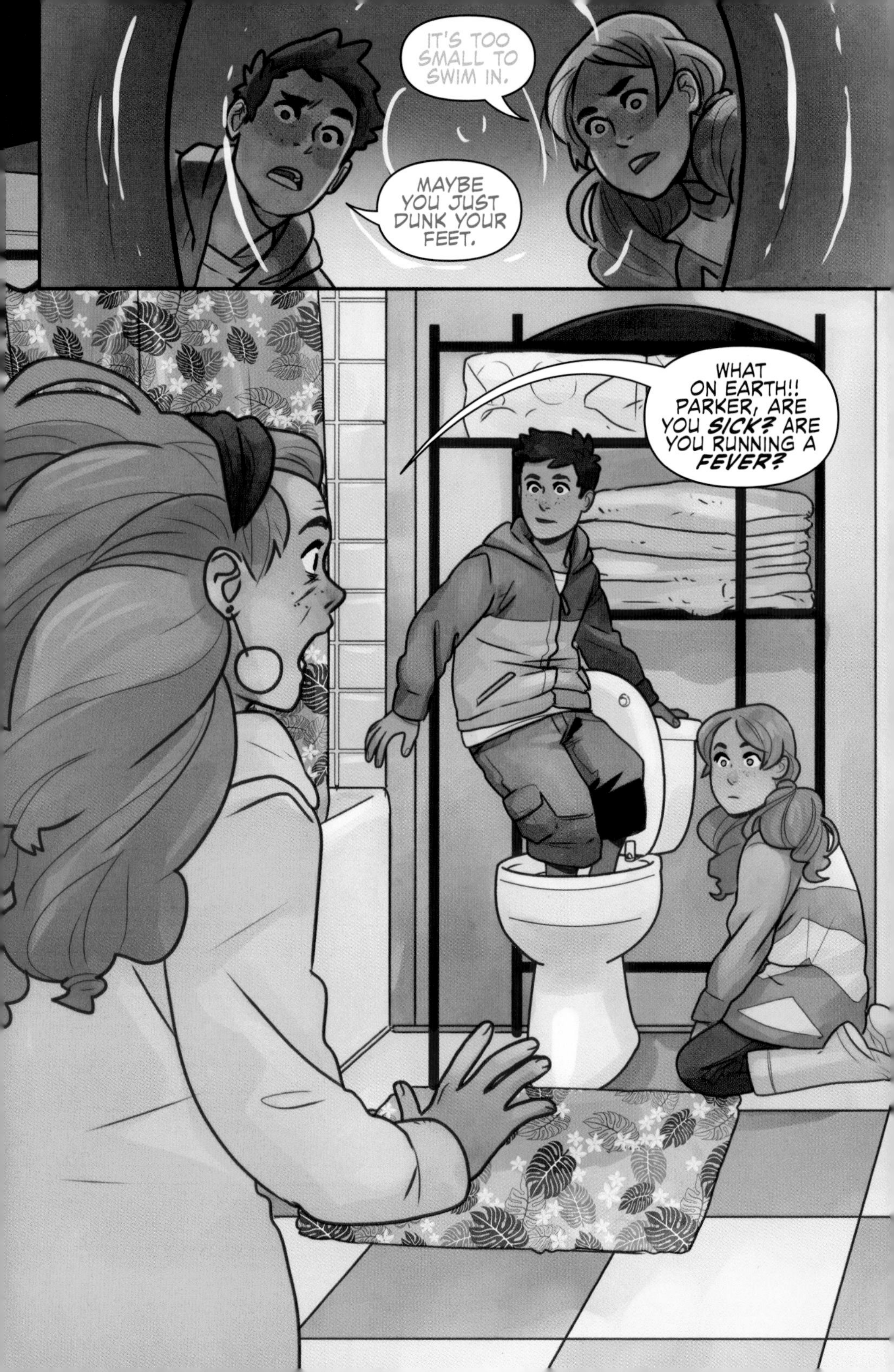
IT'S TOO SMALL TO SWIM IN.
MAYBE YOU JUST DUNK YOUR FEET.
WHAT ON EARTH!! PARKER, ARE YOU *SICK?* ARE YOU RUNNING A *FEVER?*

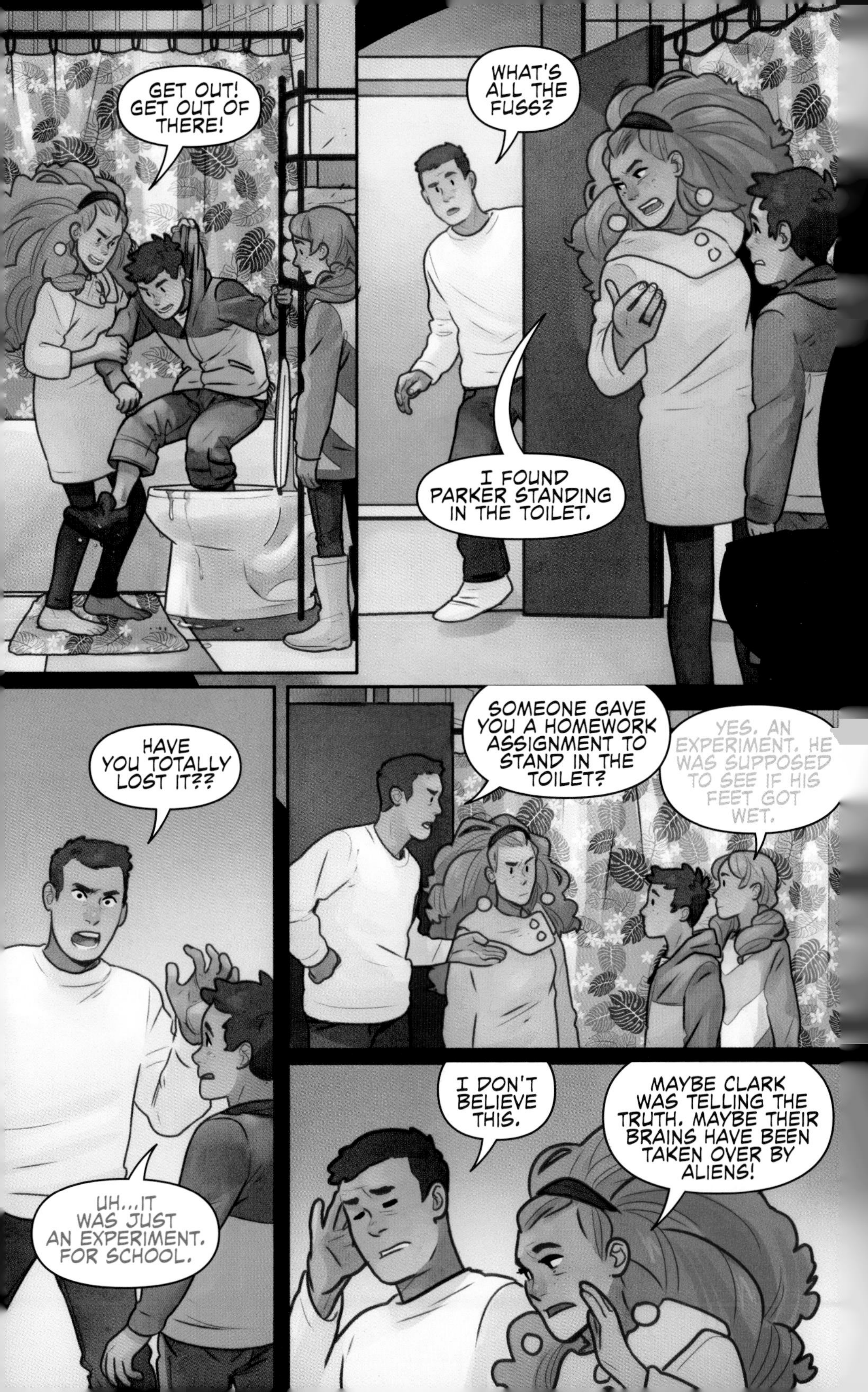
GET OUT! GET OUT OF THERE!
WHAT'S ALL THE FUSS?
I FOUND PARKER STANDING IN THE TOILET.
HAVE YOU TOTALLY LOST IT??
UH...IT WAS JUST AN EXPERIMENT. FOR SCHOOL.
SOMEONE GAVE YOU A HOMEWORK ASSIGNMENT TO STAND IN THE TOILET?
YES. AN EXPERIMENT. HE WAS SUPPOSED TO SEE IF HIS FEET GOT WET.
I DON'T BELIEVE THIS.
MAYBE CLARK WAS TELLING THE TRUTH. MAYBE THEIR BRAINS HAVE BEEN TAKEN OVER BY ALIENS!

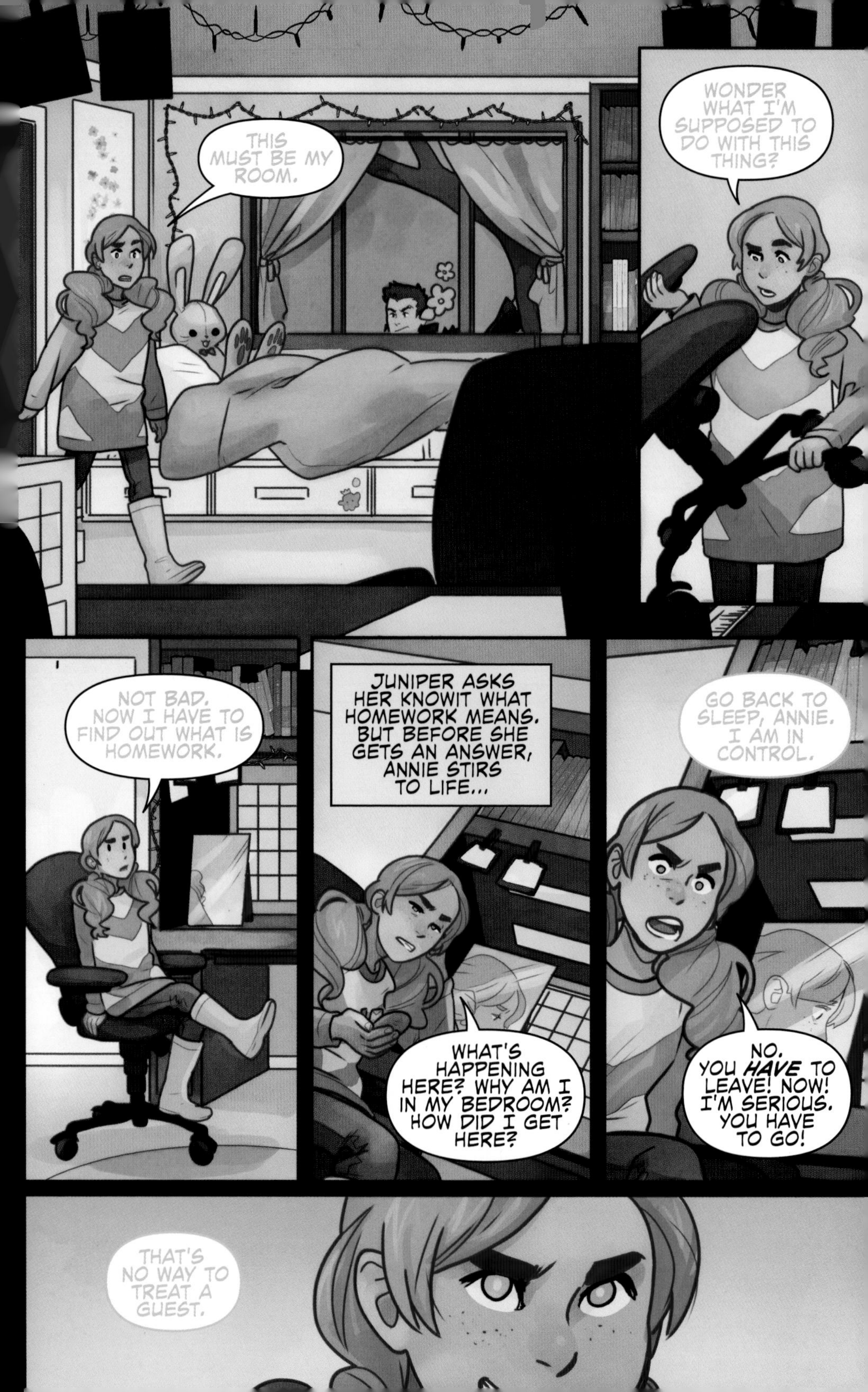

THIS MUST BE MY ROOM.
WONDER WHAT I'M SUPPOSED TO DO WITH THIS THING?
NOT BAD. NOW I HAVE TO FIND OUT WHAT IS HOMEWORK.
JUNIPER ASKS HER KNOWIT WHAT HOMEWORK MEANS. BUT BEFORE SHE GETS AN ANSWER, ANNIE STIRS TO LIFE...
WHAT'S HAPPENING HERE? WHY AM I IN MY BEDROOM? HOW DID I GET HERE?
GO BACK TO SLEEP, ANNIE. I AM IN CONTROL.
NO. YOU *HAVE* TO LEAVE! NOW! I'M SERIOUS. YOU HAVE TO GO!
THAT'S NO WAY TO TREAT A GUEST.

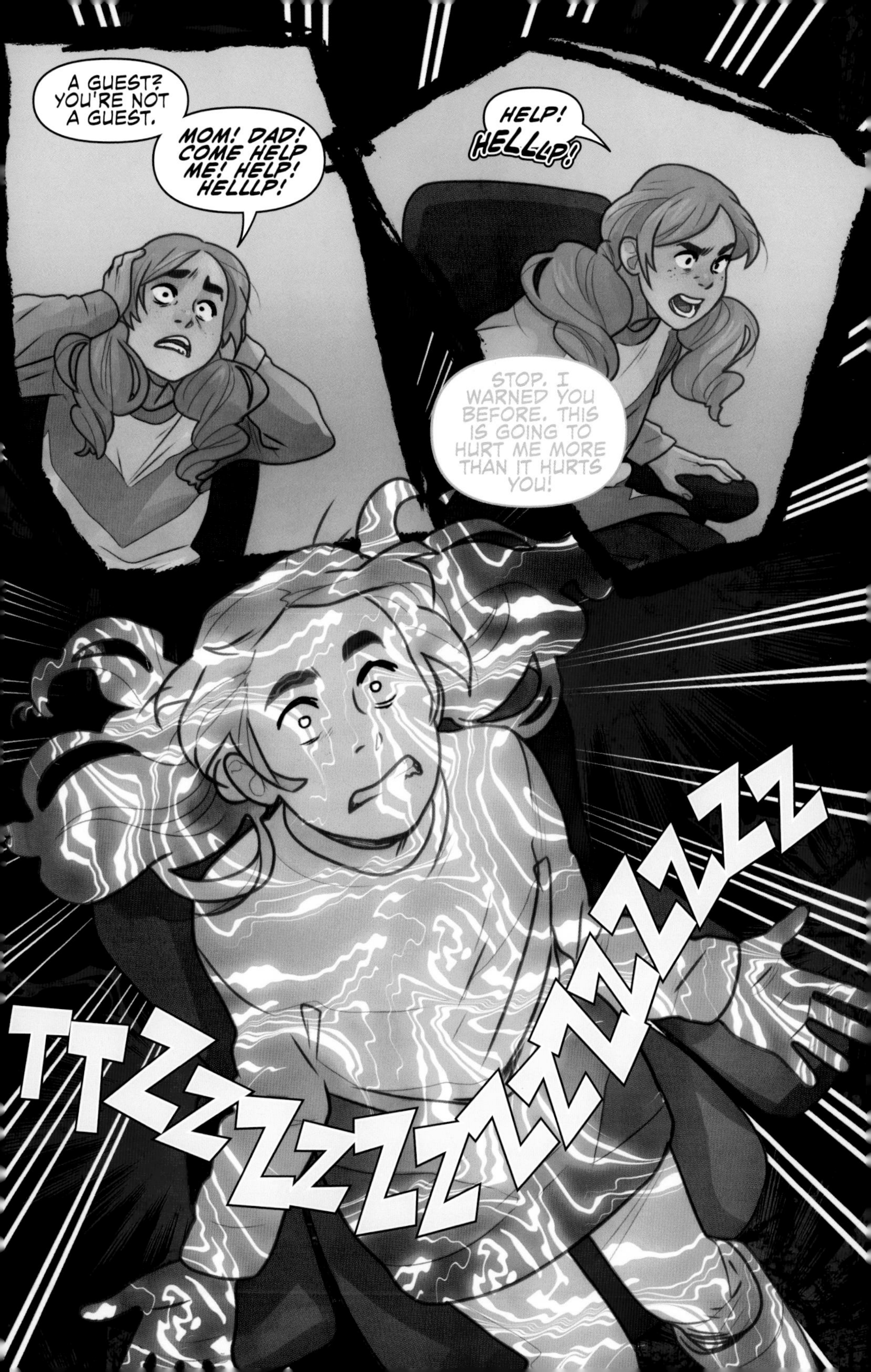
A GUEST? YOU'RE NOT A GUEST.
MOM! DAD! COME HELP ME! HELP! HELLLP!
HELP! HELLLLP!
STOP. I WARNED YOU BEFORE. THIS IS GOING TO HURT ME MORE THAN IT HURTS YOU!
TTZZZZZZZZZZZZ

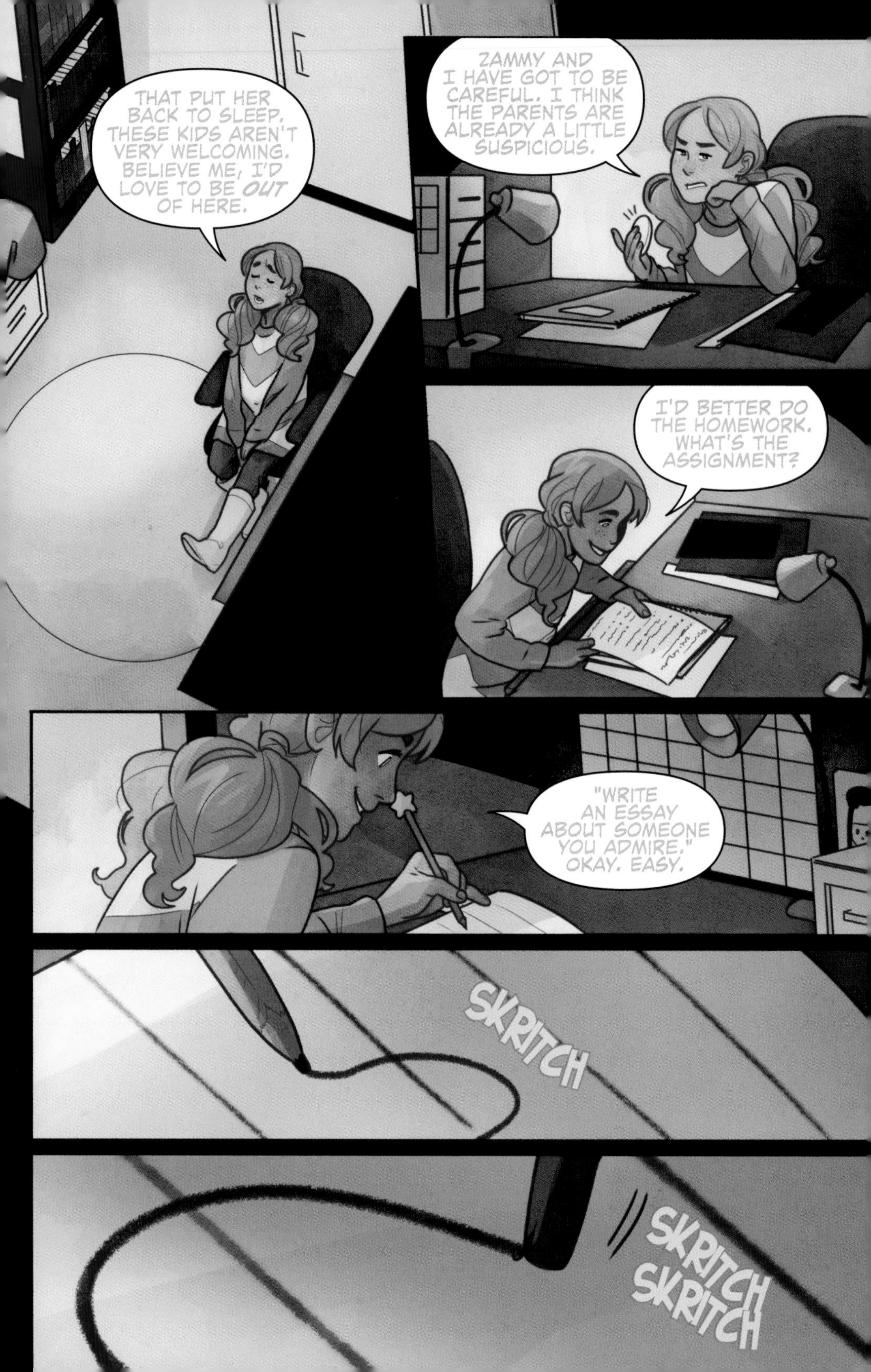
THAT PUT HER BACK TO SLEEP. THESE KIDS AREN'T VERY WELCOMING. BELIEVE ME, I'D LOVE TO BE *OUT* OF HERE.
ZAMMY AND I HAVE GOT TO BE CAREFUL. I THINK THE PARENTS ARE ALREADY A LITTLE SUSPICIOUS.
I'D BETTER DO THE HOMEWORK. WHAT'S THE ASSIGNMENT?
"WRITE AN ESSAY ABOUT SOMEONE YOU ADMIRE." OKAY. EASY.
SKRITCH
SKRITCH
SKRITCH

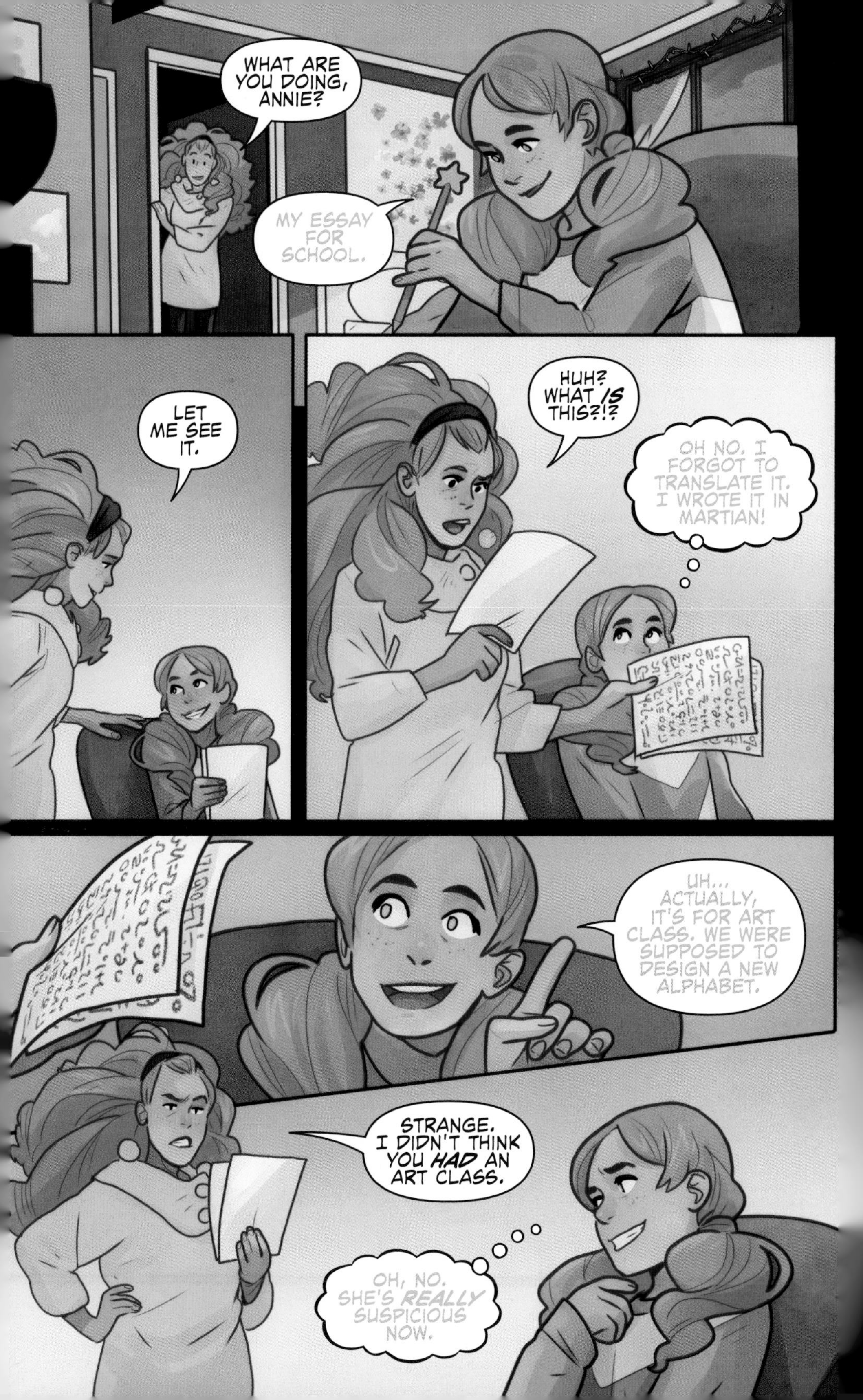
WHAT ARE YOU DOING, ANNIE?
MY ESSAY FOR SCHOOL.
LET ME SEE IT.
HUH? WHAT *IS* THIS?!?
OH NO. I FORGOT TO TRANSLATE IT. I WROTE IT IN MARTIAN!
UH... ACTUALLY, IT'S FOR ART CLASS. WE WERE SUPPOSED TO DESIGN A NEW ALPHABET.
STRANGE. I DIDN'T THINK YOU *HAD* AN ART CLASS.
OH, NO. SHE'S *REALLY* SUSPICIOUS NOW.

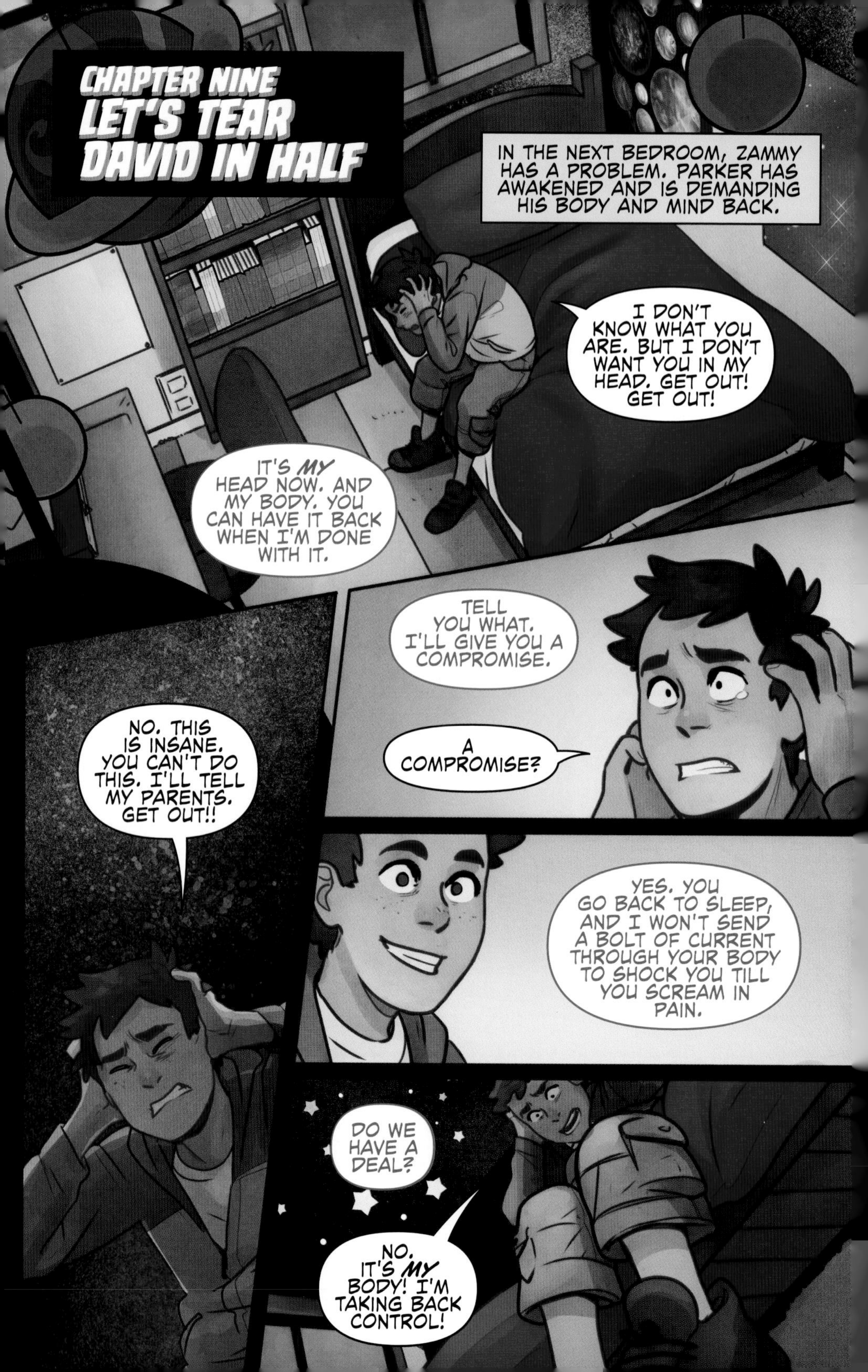
CHAPTER NINE
LET'S TEAR DAVID IN HALF
IN THE NEXT BEDROOM, ZAMMY HAS A PROBLEM. PARKER HAS AWAKENED AND IS DEMANDING HIS BODY AND MIND BACK.
I DON'T KNOW WHAT YOU ARE. BUT I DON'T WANT YOU IN MY HEAD. GET OUT! GET OUT!
IT'S MY HEAD NOW. AND MY BODY. YOU CAN HAVE IT BACK WHEN I'M DONE WITH IT.
NO. THIS IS INSANE. YOU CAN'T DO THIS. I'LL TELL MY PARENTS. GET OUT!!
TELL YOU WHAT. I'LL GIVE YOU A COMPROMISE.
A COMPROMISE?
YES. YOU GO BACK TO SLEEP, AND I WON'T SEND A BOLT OF CURRENT THROUGH YOUR BODY TO SHOCK YOU TILL YOU SCREAM IN PAIN.
DO WE HAVE A DEAL?
NO. IT'S MY BODY! I'M TAKING BACK CONTROL!

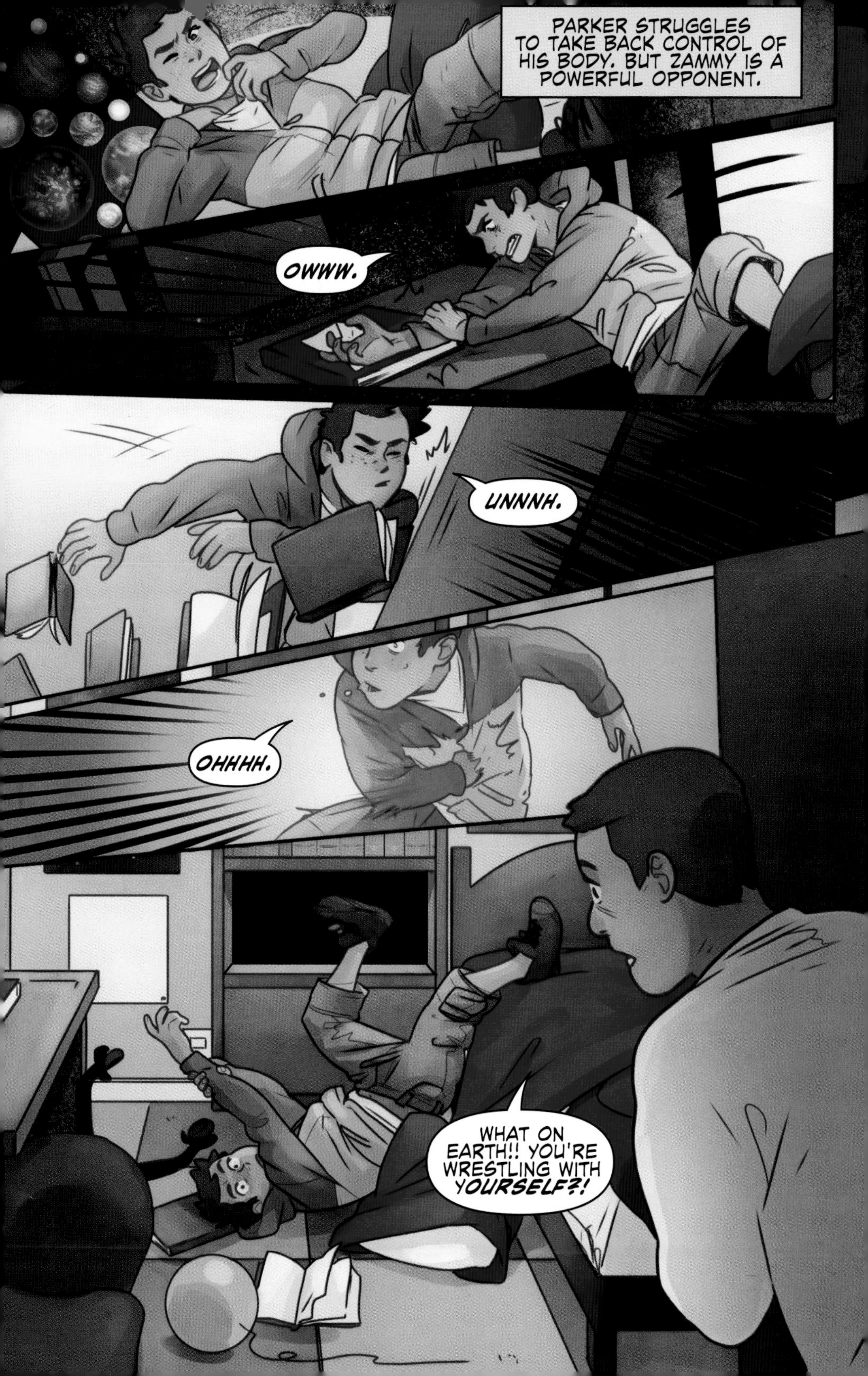
PARKER STRUGGLES TO TAKE BACK CONTROL OF HIS BODY. BUT ZAMMY IS A POWERFUL OPPONENT.
OWWW.
UNNNH.
OHHHH.
WHAT ON EARTH!! YOU'RE WRESTLING WITH YOURSELF?!

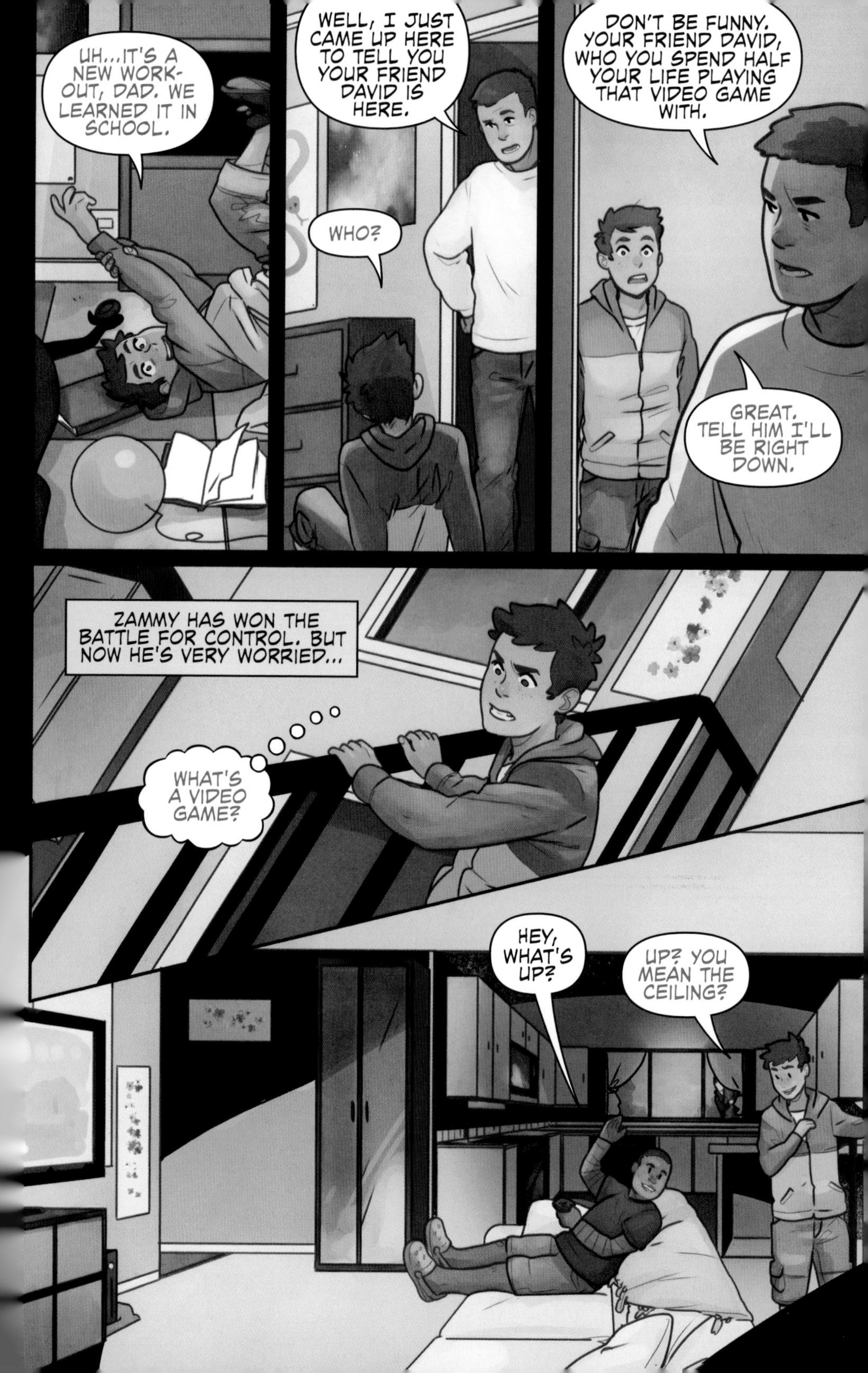
UH...IT'S A NEW WORK-OUT, DAD. WE LEARNED IT IN SCHOOL.
WELL, I JUST CAME UP HERE TO TELL YOU YOUR FRIEND DAVID IS HERE.
WHO?
DON'T BE FUNNY. YOUR FRIEND DAVID, WHO YOU SPEND HALF YOUR LIFE PLAYING THAT VIDEO GAME WITH.
GREAT. TELL HIM I'LL BE RIGHT DOWN.
ZAMMY HAS WON THE BATTLE FOR CONTROL. BUT NOW HE'S VERY WORRIED...
WHAT'S A VIDEO GAME?
HEY, WHAT'S UP?
UP? YOU MEAN THE CEILING?

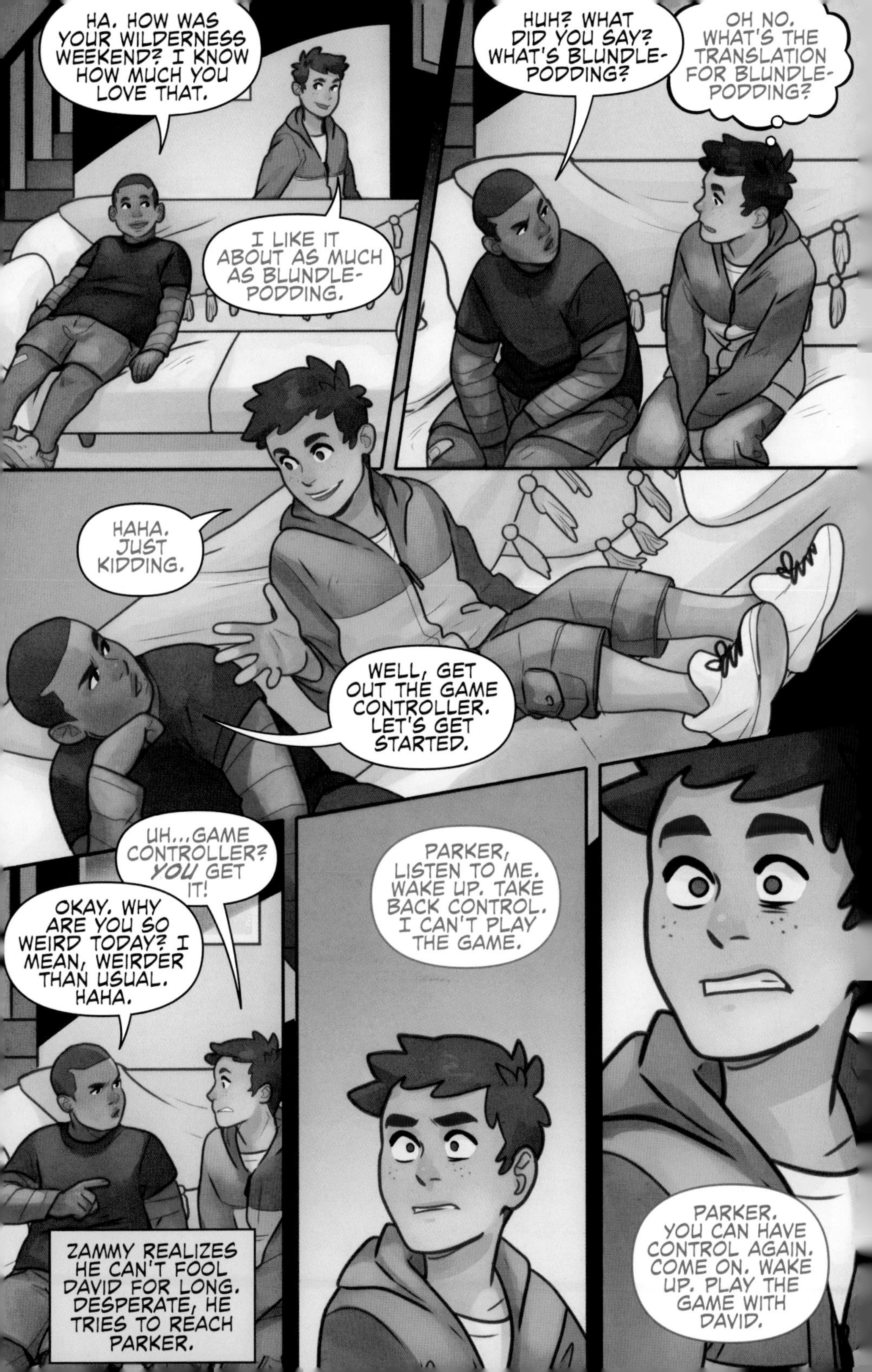
HA. HOW WAS YOUR WILDERNESS WEEKEND? I KNOW HOW MUCH YOU LOVE THAT.
I LIKE IT ABOUT AS MUCH AS BLUNDLE-PODDING.
HUH? WHAT DID YOU SAY? WHAT'S BLUNDLE-PODDING?
OH NO. WHAT'S THE TRANSLATION FOR BLUNDLE-PODDING?
HAHA. JUST KIDDING.
WELL, GET OUT THE GAME CONTROLLER. LET'S GET STARTED.
UH...GAME CONTROLLER? YOU GET IT!
OKAY. WHY ARE YOU SO WEIRD TODAY? I MEAN, WEIRDER THAN USUAL. HAHA.
ZAMMY REALIZES HE CAN'T FOOL DAVID FOR LONG. DESPERATE, HE TRIES TO REACH PARKER.
PARKER, LISTEN TO ME. WAKE UP. TAKE BACK CONTROL. I CAN'T PLAY THE GAME.
PARKER. YOU CAN HAVE CONTROL AGAIN. COME ON. WAKE UP. PLAY THE GAME WITH DAVID.

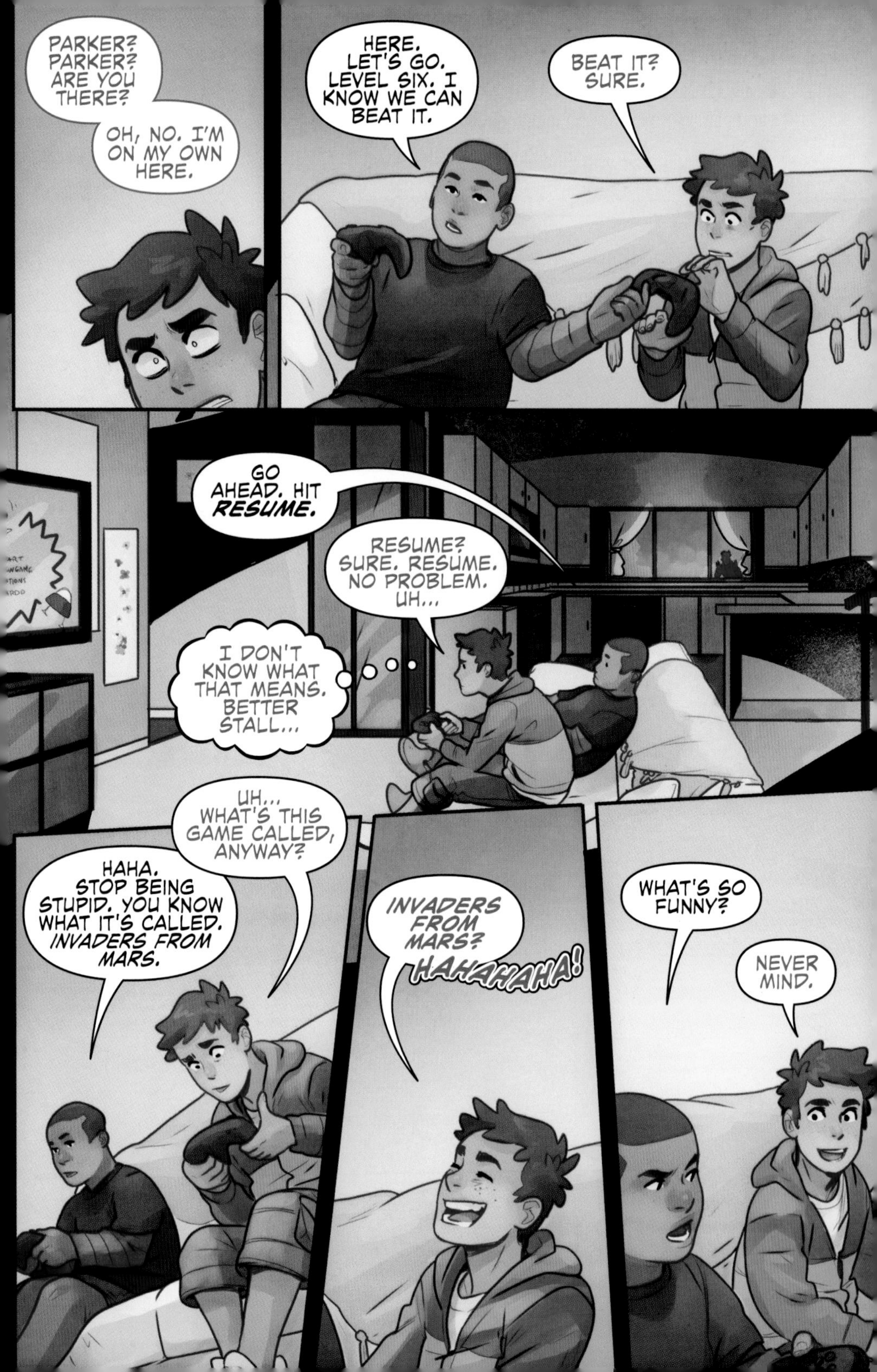
PARKER? PARKER? ARE YOU THERE?
OH, NO. I'M ON MY OWN HERE.
HERE. LET'S GO. LEVEL SIX. I KNOW WE CAN BEAT IT.
BEAT IT? SURE.
GO AHEAD. HIT *RESUME.*
RESUME? SURE. RESUME. NO PROBLEM. UH...
I DON'T KNOW WHAT THAT MEANS. BETTER STALL...
UH... WHAT'S THIS GAME CALLED, ANYWAY?
HAHA. STOP BEING STUPID. YOU KNOW WHAT IT'S CALLED. *INVADERS FROM MARS.*
INVADERS FROM MARS?
HAHAHAHA!
WHAT'S SO FUNNY?
NEVER MIND.

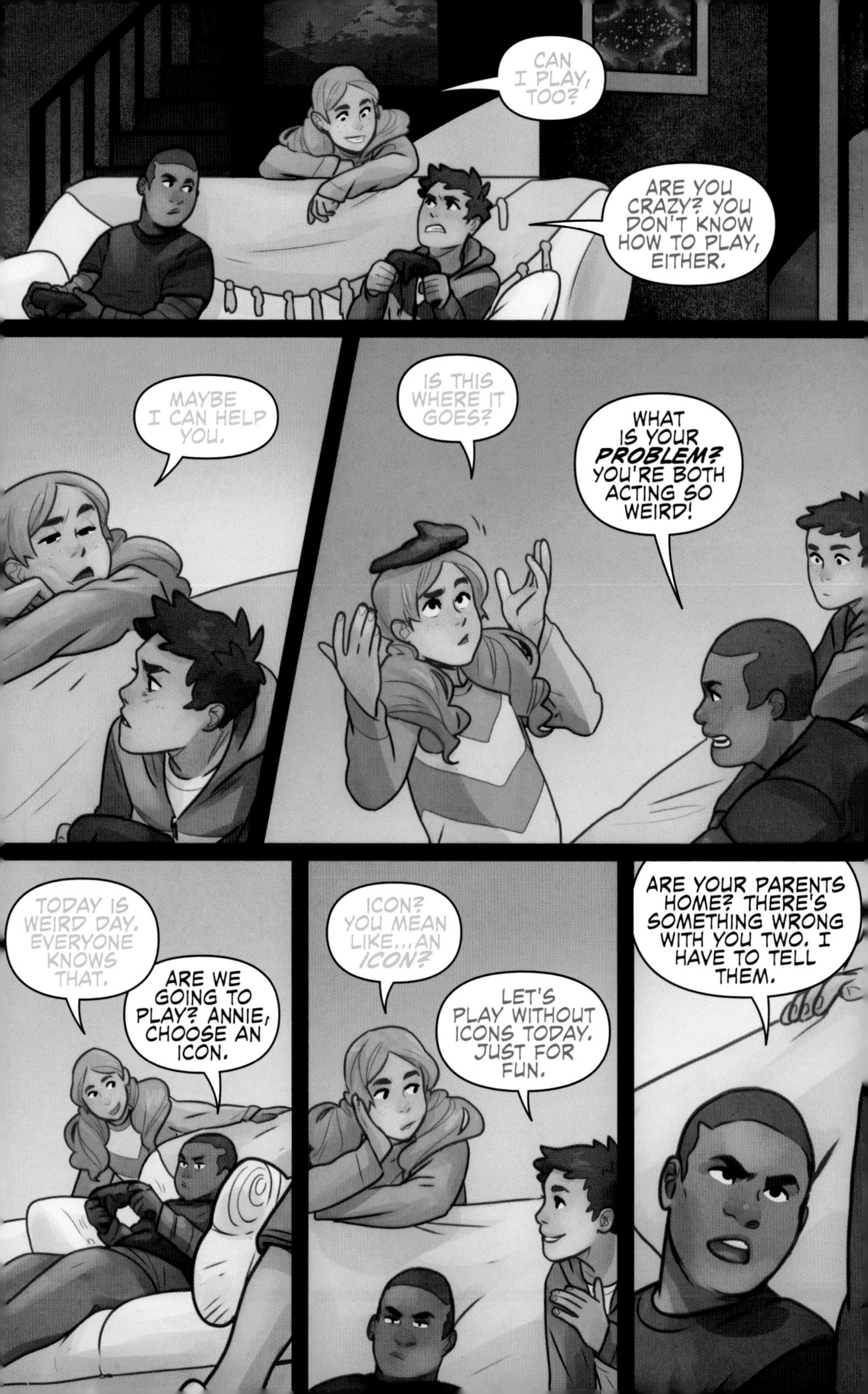
CAN I PLAY, TOO?
ARE YOU CRAZY? YOU DON'T KNOW HOW TO PLAY, EITHER.
MAYBE I CAN HELP YOU.
IS THIS WHERE IT GOES?
WHAT IS YOUR PROBLEM? YOU'RE BOTH ACTING SO WEIRD!
TODAY IS WEIRD DAY. EVERYONE KNOWS THAT.
ARE WE GOING TO PLAY? ANNIE, CHOOSE AN ICON.
ICON? YOU MEAN LIKE...AN ICON?
LET'S PLAY WITHOUT ICONS TODAY. JUST FOR FUN.
ARE YOUR PARENTS HOME? THERE'S SOMETHING WRONG WITH YOU TWO. I HAVE TO TELL THEM.

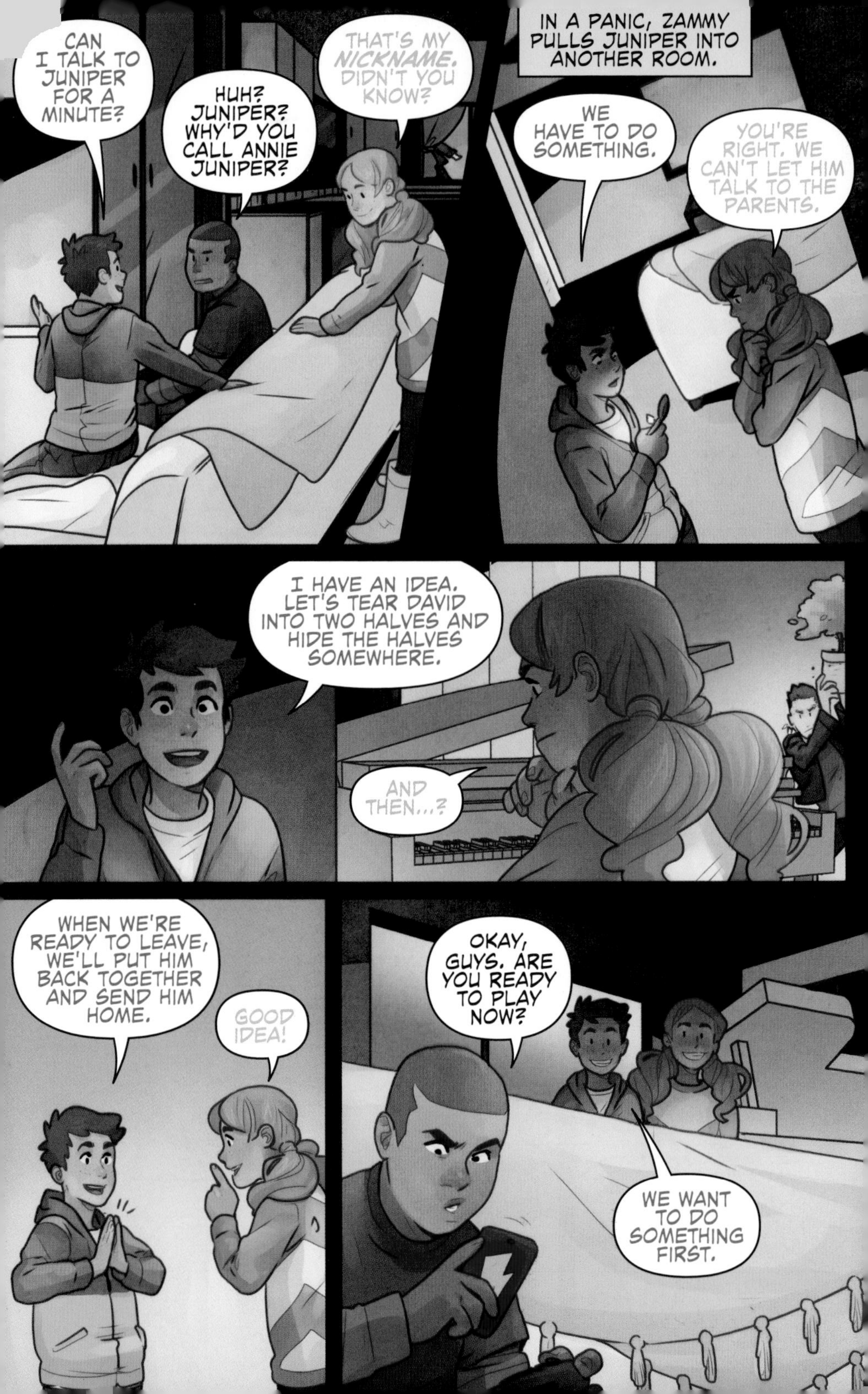
CAN I TALK TO JUNIPER FOR A MINUTE?
HUH? JUNIPER? WHY'D YOU CALL ANNIE JUNIPER?
THAT'S MY *NICKNAME.* DIDN'T YOU KNOW?
IN A PANIC, ZAMMY PULLS JUNIPER INTO ANOTHER ROOM.
WE HAVE TO DO SOMETHING.
YOU'RE RIGHT. WE CAN'T LET HIM TALK TO THE PARENTS.
I HAVE AN IDEA. LET'S TEAR DAVID INTO TWO HALVES AND HIDE THE HALVES SOMEWHERE.
AND THEN...?
WHEN WE'RE READY TO LEAVE, WE'LL PUT HIM BACK TOGETHER AND SEND HIM HOME.
GOOD IDEA!
OKAY, GUYS. ARE YOU READY TO PLAY NOW?
WE WANT TO DO SOMETHING FIRST.

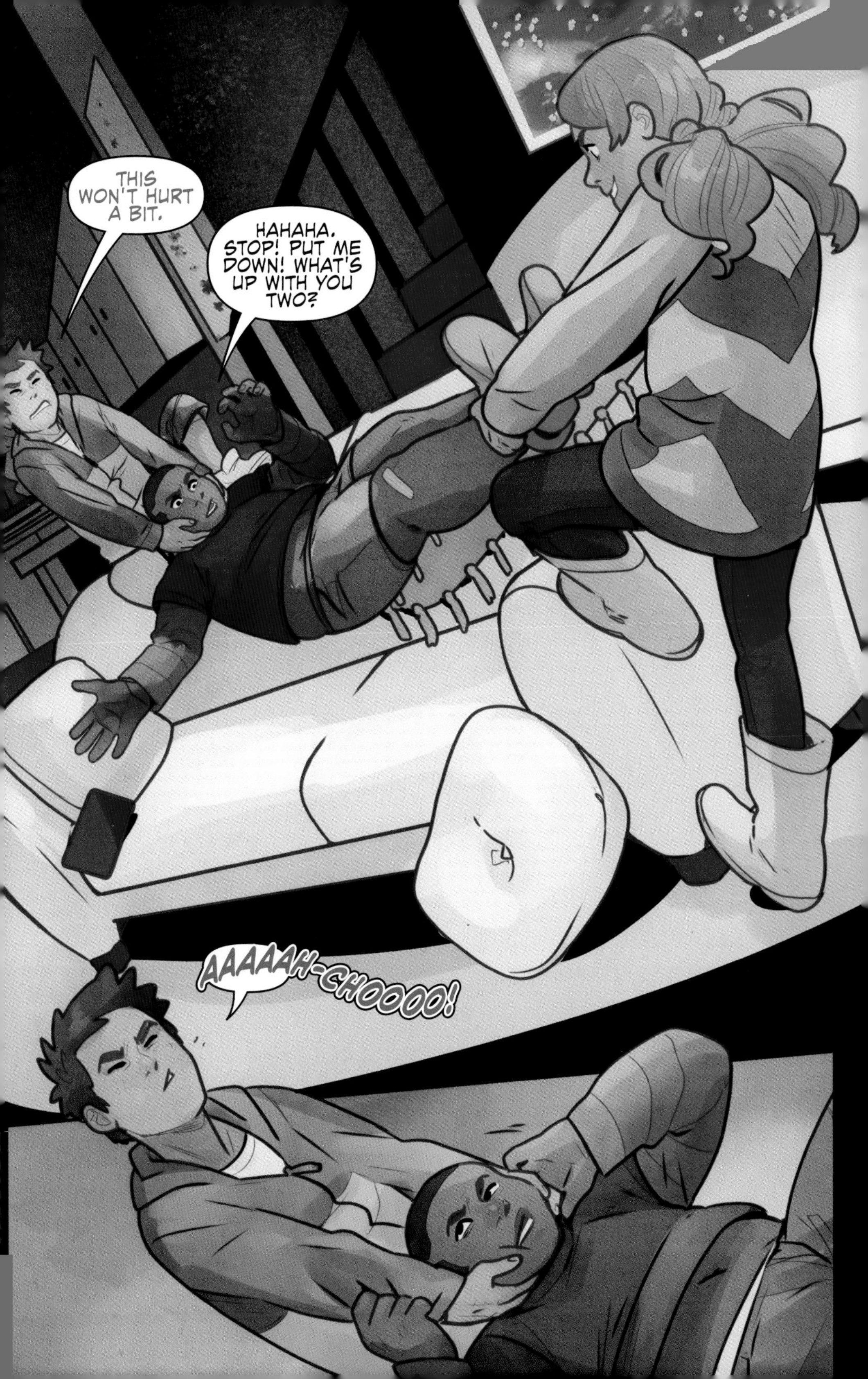
THIS WON'T HURT A BIT.
HAHAHA. STOP! PUT ME DOWN! WHAT'S UP WITH YOU TWO?
AAAAAH-CHOOOOO!

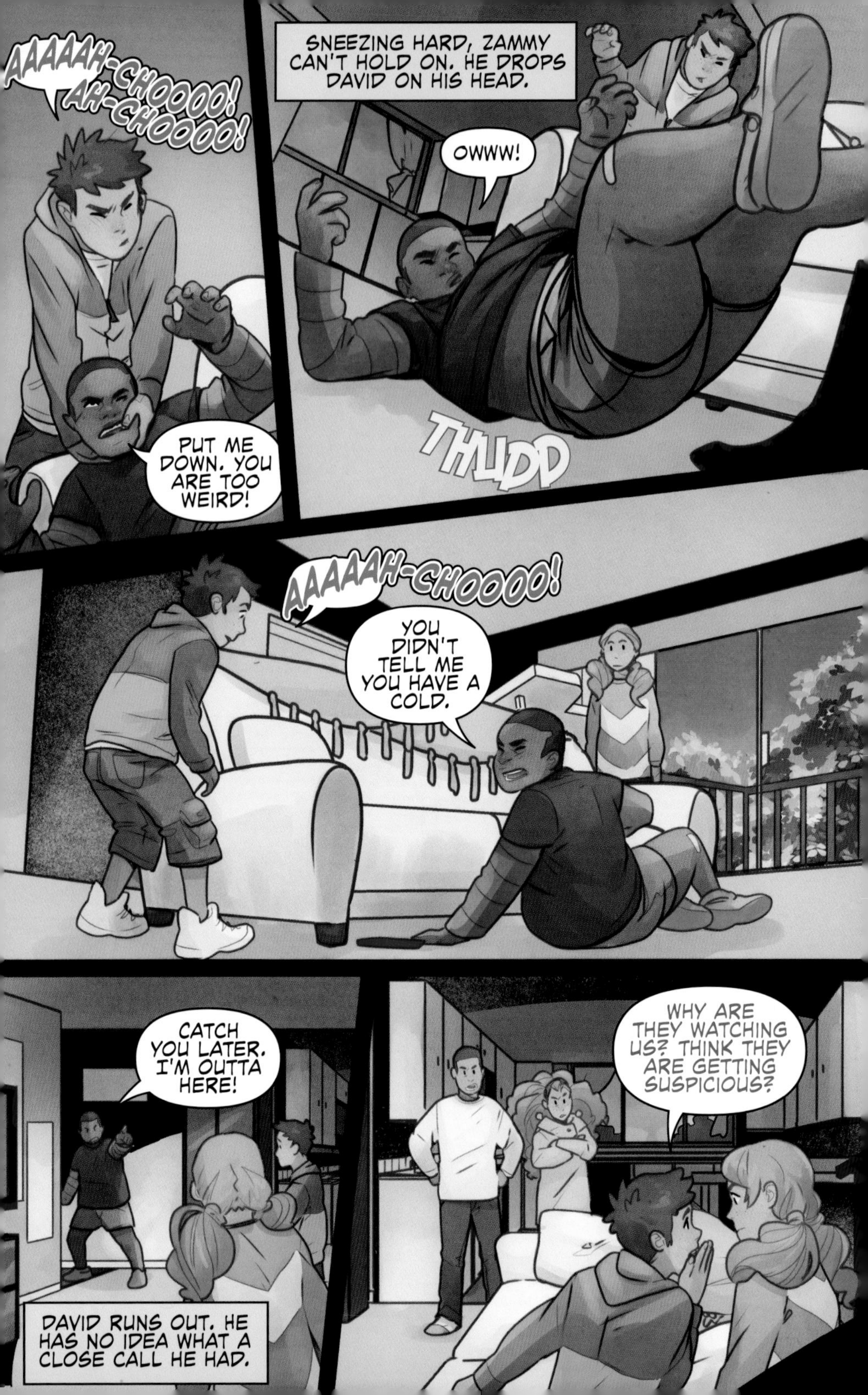
AAAAAH-CHOOOOO!
AH-CHOOOOO!
PUT ME DOWN. YOU ARE TOO WEIRD!
SNEEZING HARD, ZAMMY CAN'T HOLD ON. HE DROPS DAVID ON HIS HEAD.
OWWW!
THUDD
AAAAAH-CHOOOOO!
YOU DIDN'T TELL ME YOU HAVE A COLD.
CATCH YOU LATER. I'M OUTTA HERE!
DAVID RUNS OUT. HE HAS NO IDEA WHAT A CLOSE CALL HE HAD.
WHY ARE THEY WATCHING US? THINK THEY ARE GETTING SUSPICIOUS?

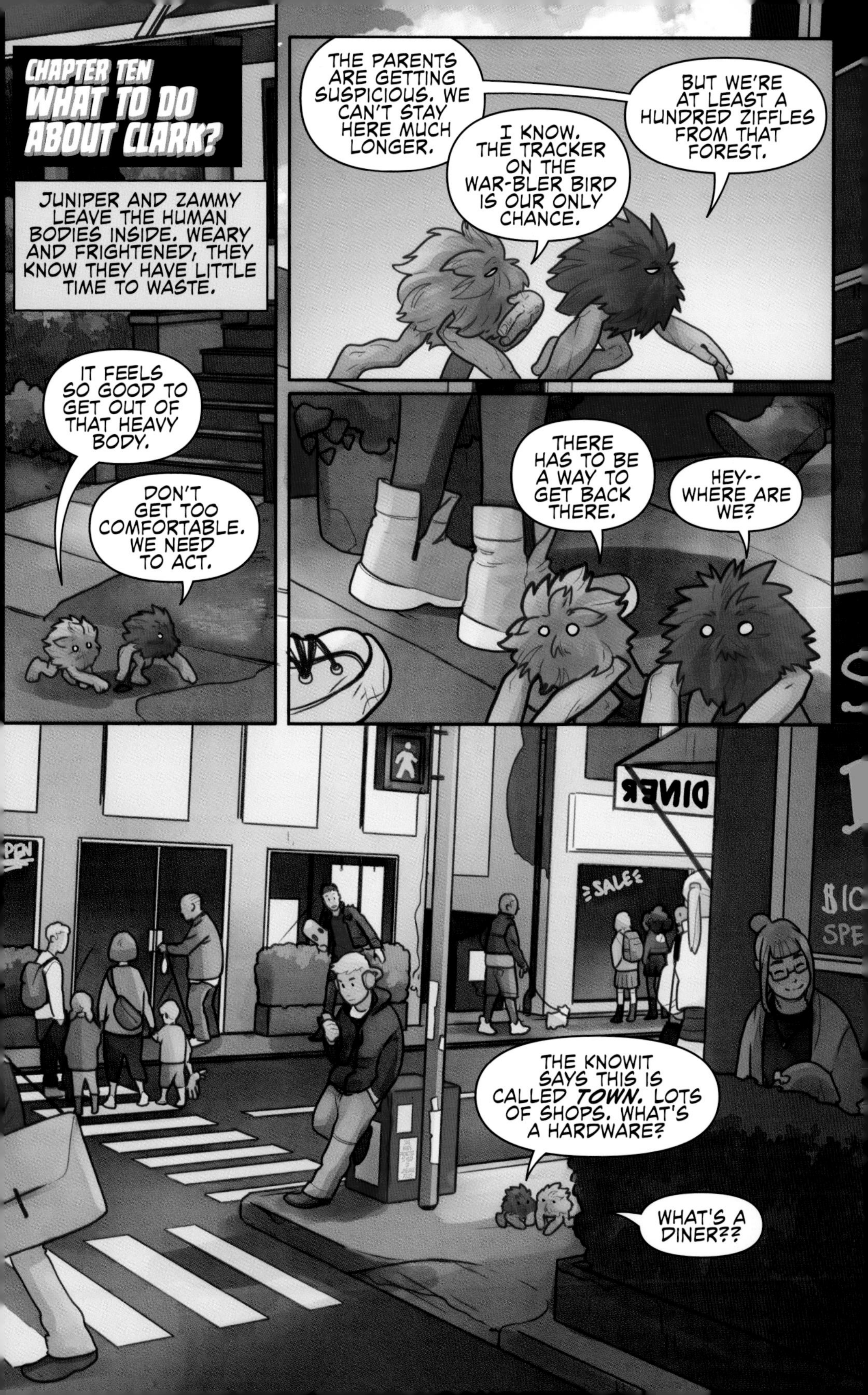
CHAPTER TEN
WHAT TO DO ABOUT CLARK?
JUNIPER AND ZAMMY LEAVE THE HUMAN BODIES INSIDE. WEARY AND FRIGHTENED, THEY KNOW THEY HAVE LITTLE TIME TO WASTE.
THE PARENTS ARE GETTING SUSPICIOUS. WE CAN'T STAY HERE MUCH LONGER.
I KNOW. THE TRACKER ON THE WAR-BLER BIRD IS OUR ONLY CHANCE.
BUT WE'RE AT LEAST A HUNDRED ZIFFLES FROM THAT FOREST.
IT FEELS SO GOOD TO GET OUT OF THAT HEAVY BODY.
DON'T GET TOO COMFORTABLE. WE NEED TO ACT.
THERE HAS TO BE A WAY TO GET BACK THERE.
HEY-- WHERE ARE WE?
DINER
SALE
THE KNOWIT SAYS THIS IS CALLED *TOWN.* LOTS OF SHOPS. WHAT'S A HARDWARE?
WHAT'S A DINER??

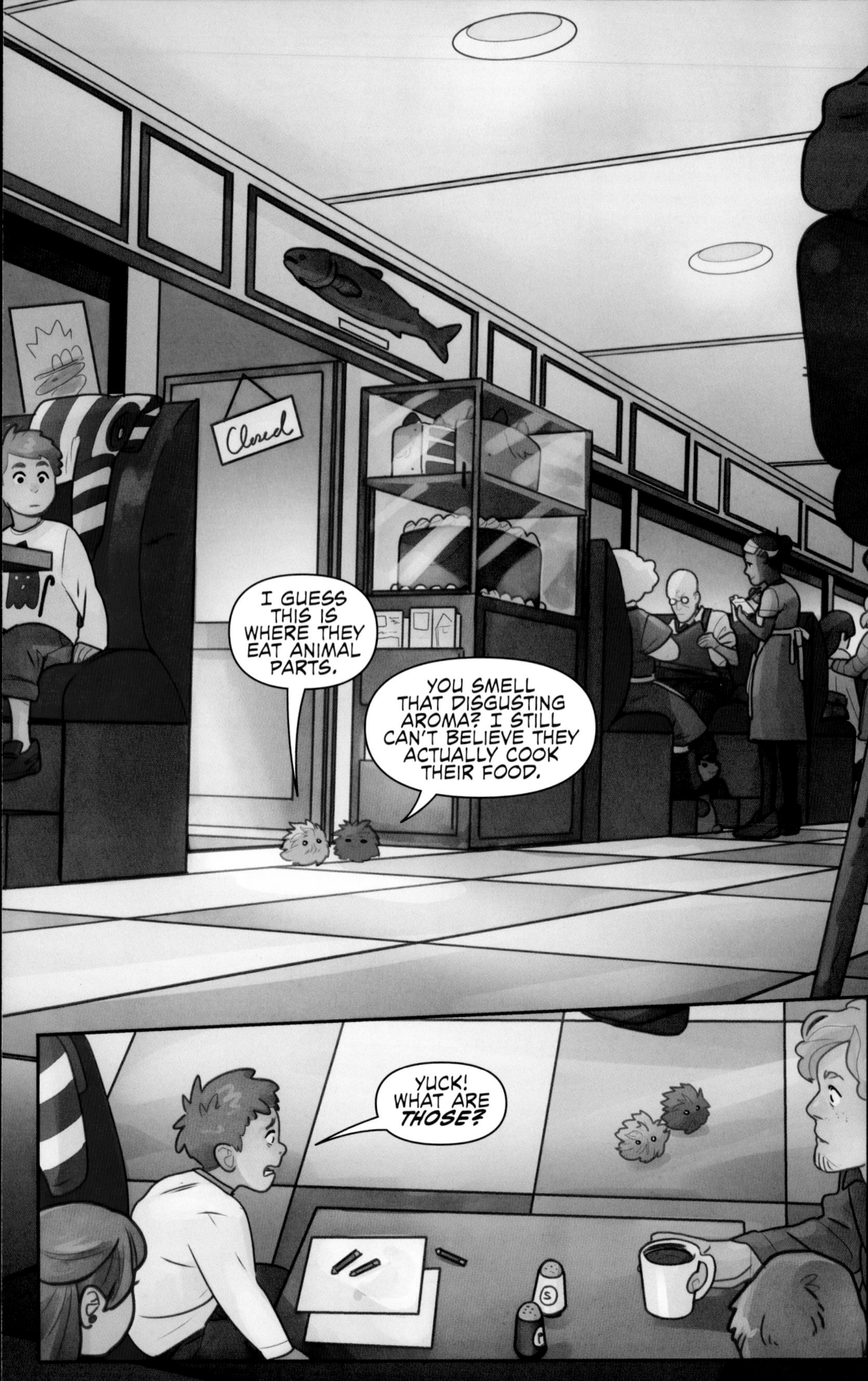
Closed
I GUESS THIS IS WHERE THEY EAT ANIMAL PARTS.
YOU SMELL THAT DISGUSTING AROMA? I STILL CAN'T BELIEVE THEY ACTUALLY COOK THEIR FOOD.
YUCK! WHAT ARE *THOSE?*

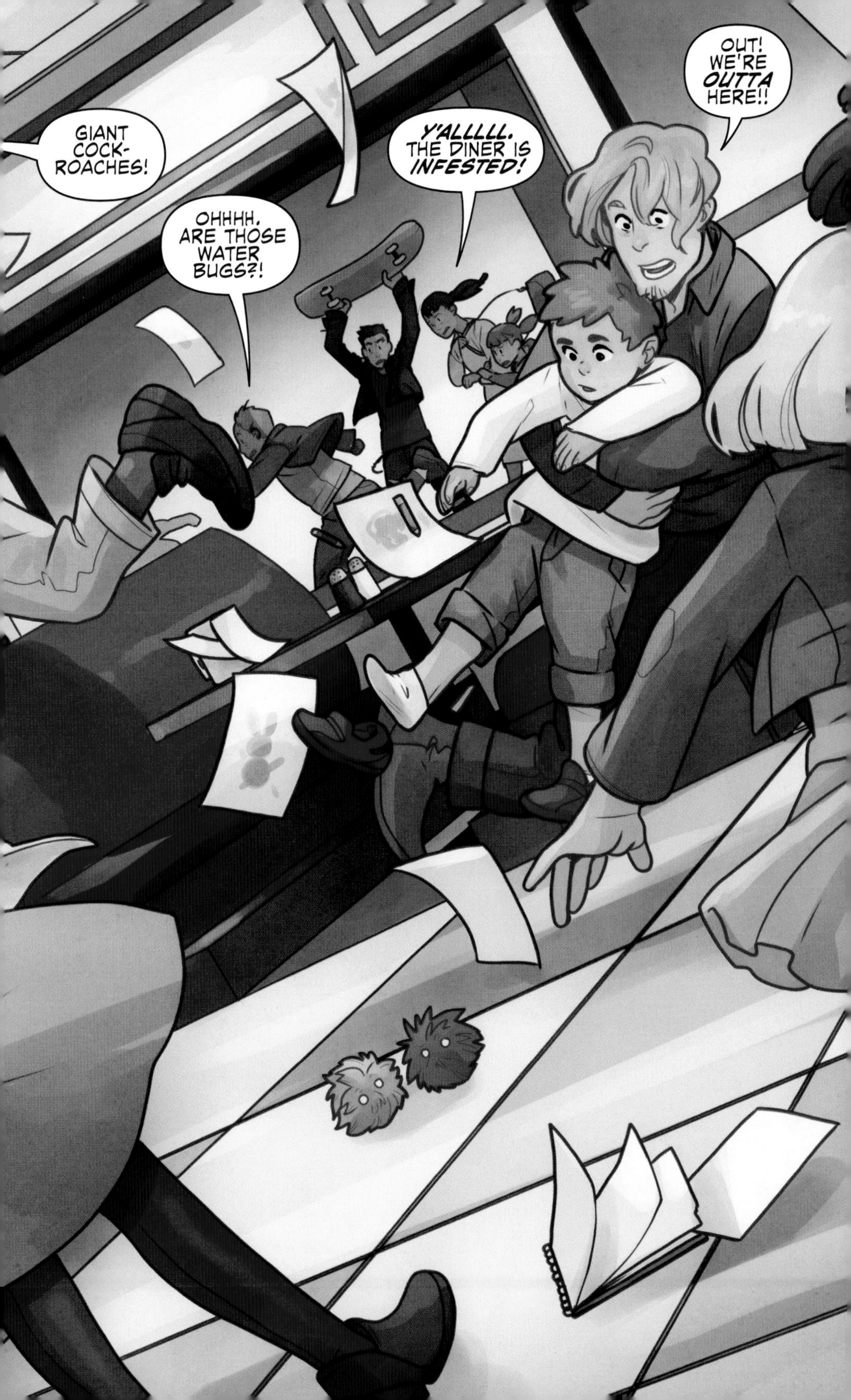
GIANT COCK-ROACHES!
OHHHH. ARE THOSE WATER BUGS?!
Y'ALLLLL. THE DINER IS INFESTED!
OUT! WE'RE OUTTA HERE!!

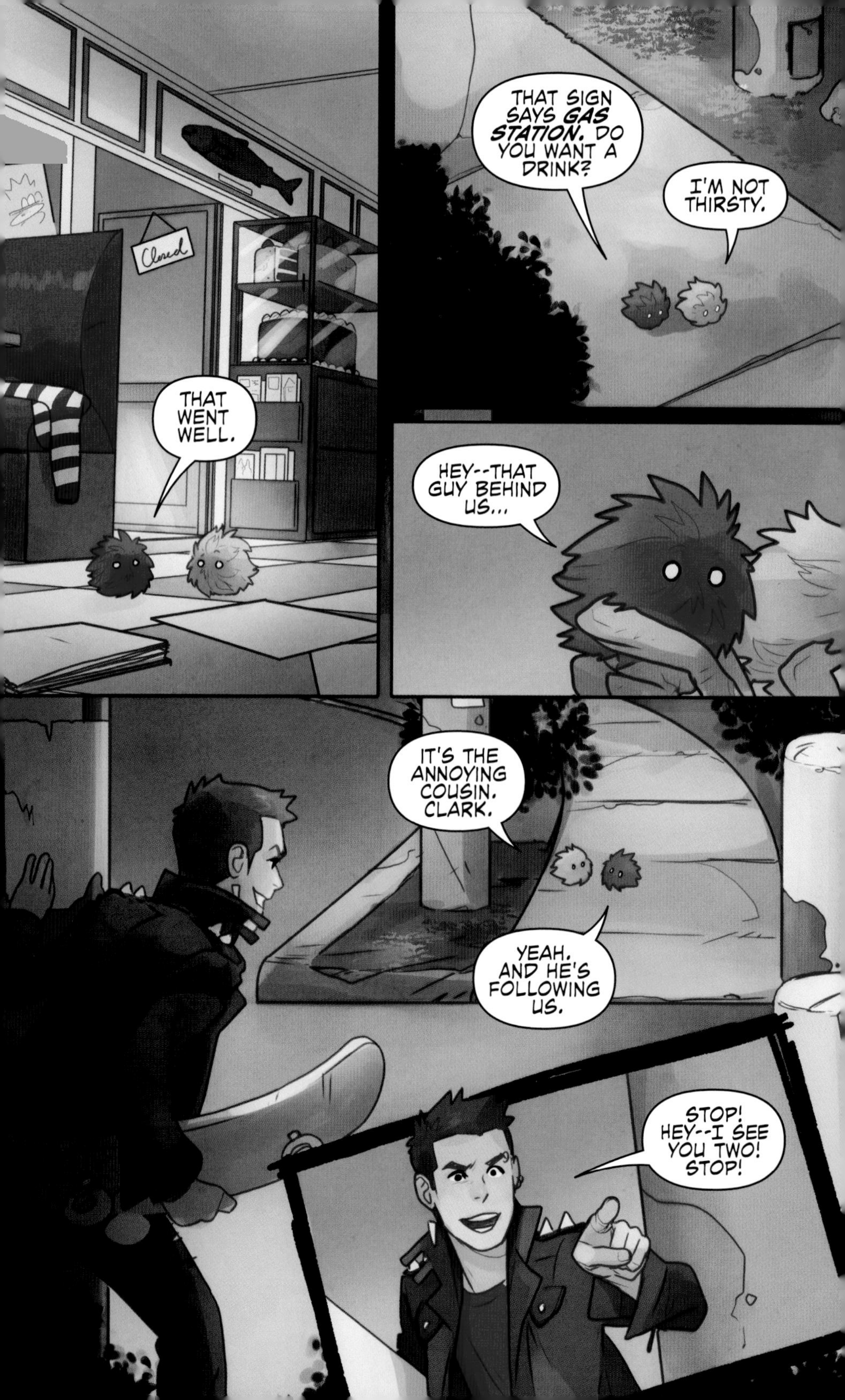
Closed
THAT WENT WELL.
THAT SIGN SAYS GAS STATION. DO YOU WANT A DRINK?
I'M NOT THIRSTY.
HEY--THAT GUY BEHIND US...
IT'S THE ANNOYING COUSIN. CLARK.
YEAH. AND HE'S FOLLOWING US.
STOP! HEY--I SEE YOU TWO! STOP!

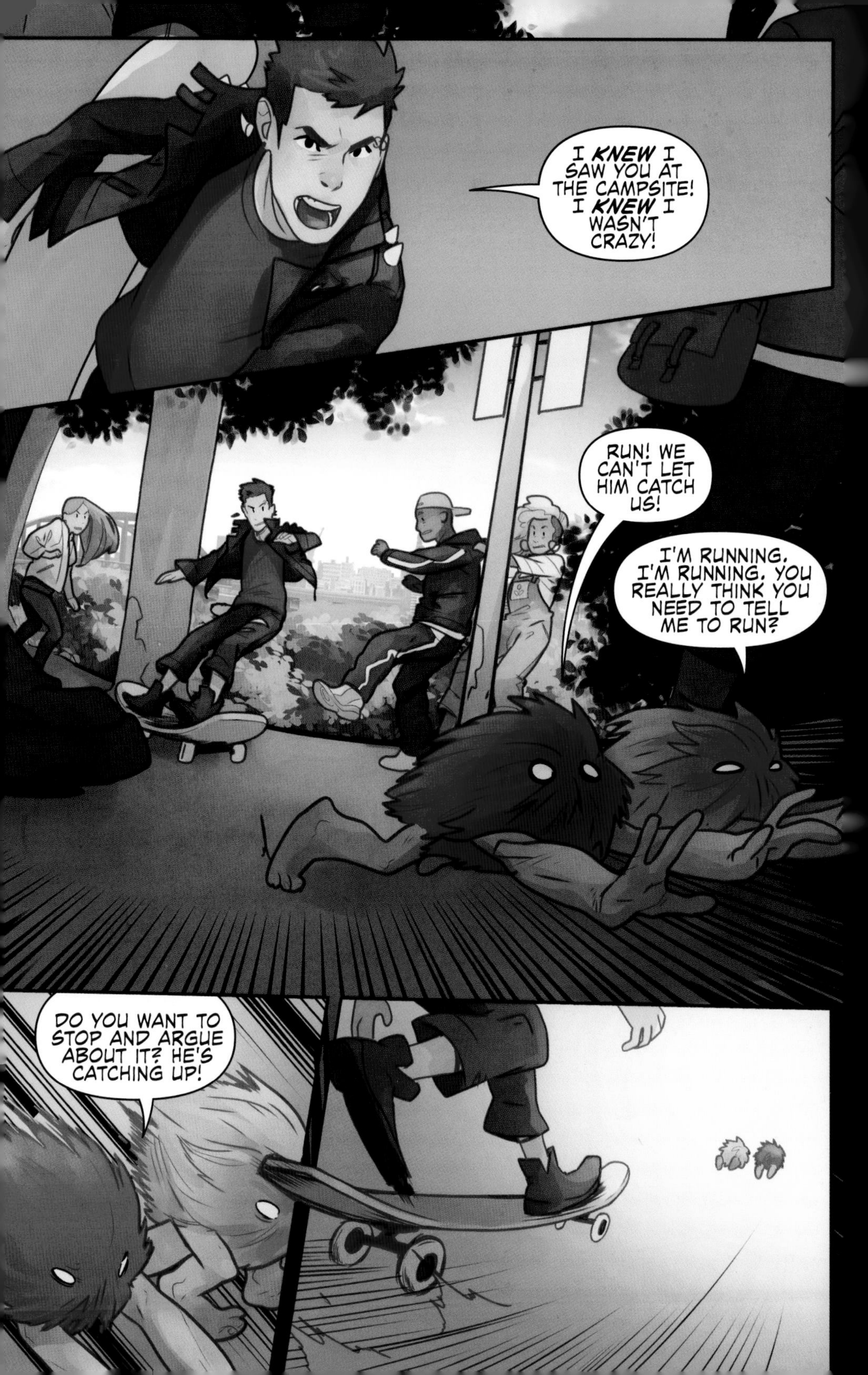
I *KNEW* I SAW YOU AT THE CAMPSITE! I *KNEW* I WASN'T CRAZY!
RUN! WE CAN'T LET HIM CATCH US!
I'M RUNNING, I'M RUNNING. YOU REALLY THINK YOU NEED TO TELL ME TO RUN?
DO YOU WANT TO STOP AND ARGUE ABOUT IT? HE'S CATCHING UP!

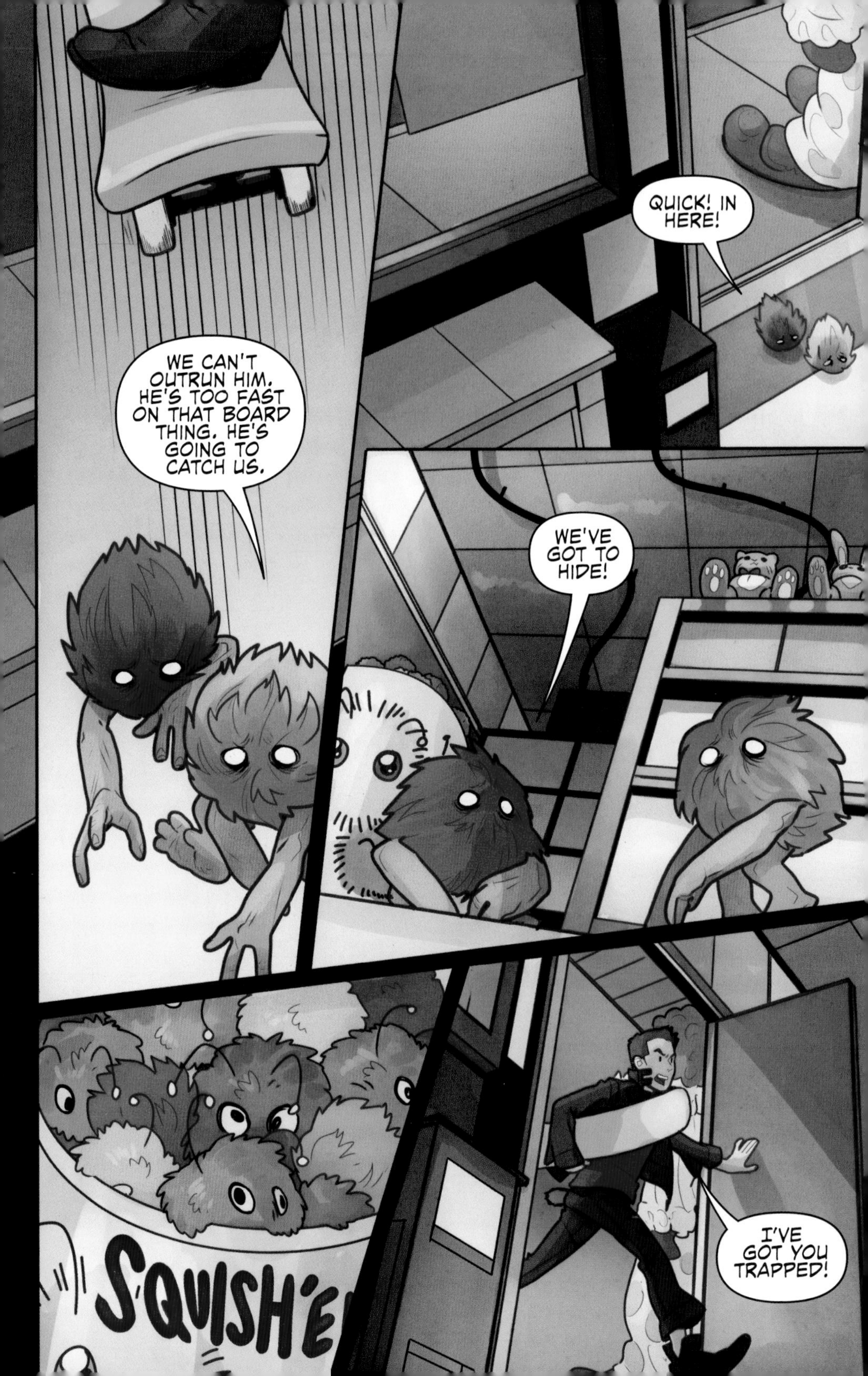
QUICK! IN HERE!
WE CAN'T OUTRUN HIM. HE'S TOO FAST ON THAT BOARD THING. HE'S GOING TO CATCH US.
WE'VE GOT TO HIDE!
I'VE GOT YOU TRAPPED!
SQUISH'E

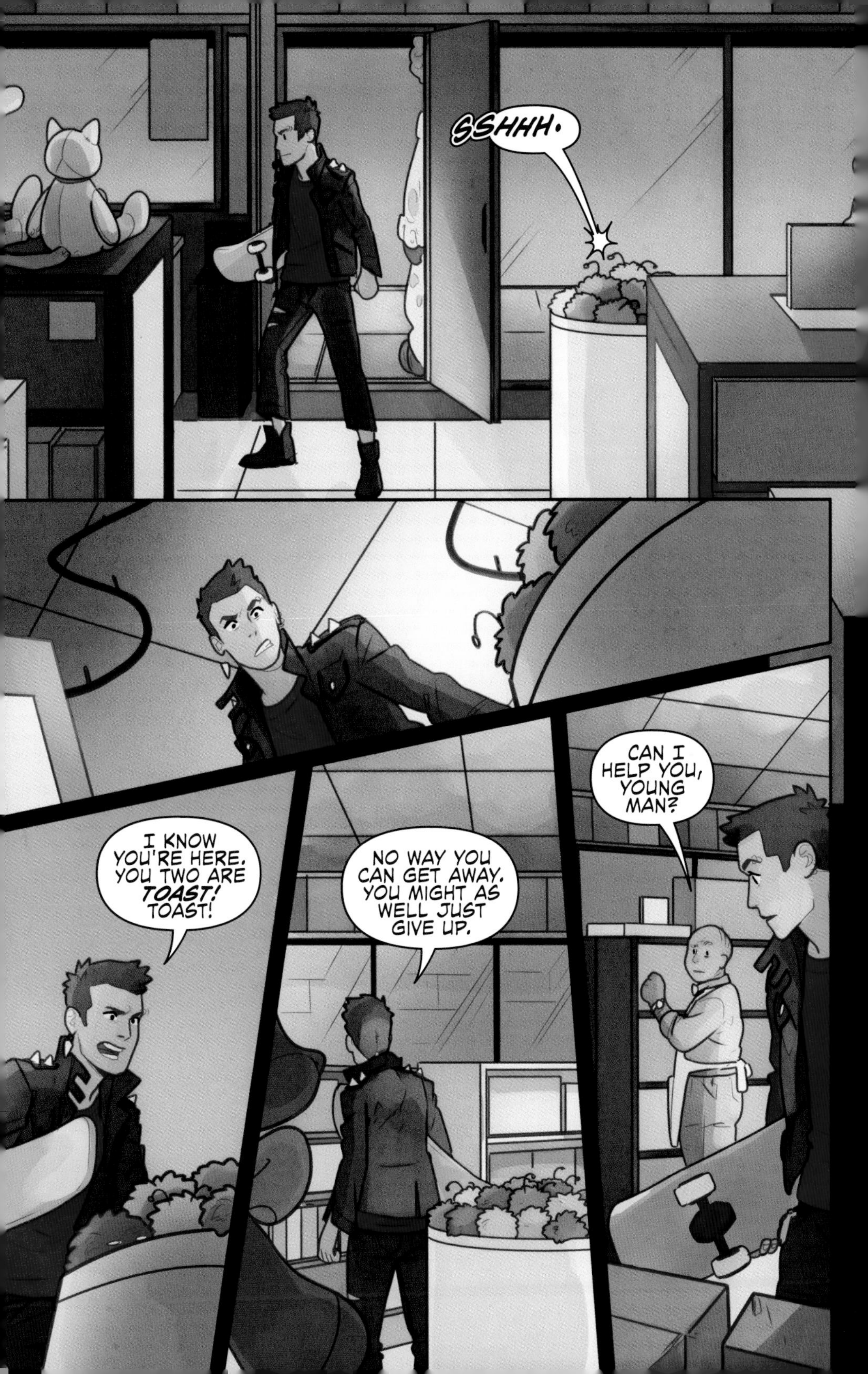
SSHHH.
I KNOW YOU'RE HERE. YOU TWO ARE *TOAST!* TOAST!
NO WAY YOU CAN GET AWAY. YOU MIGHT AS WELL JUST GIVE UP.
CAN I HELP YOU, YOUNG MAN?

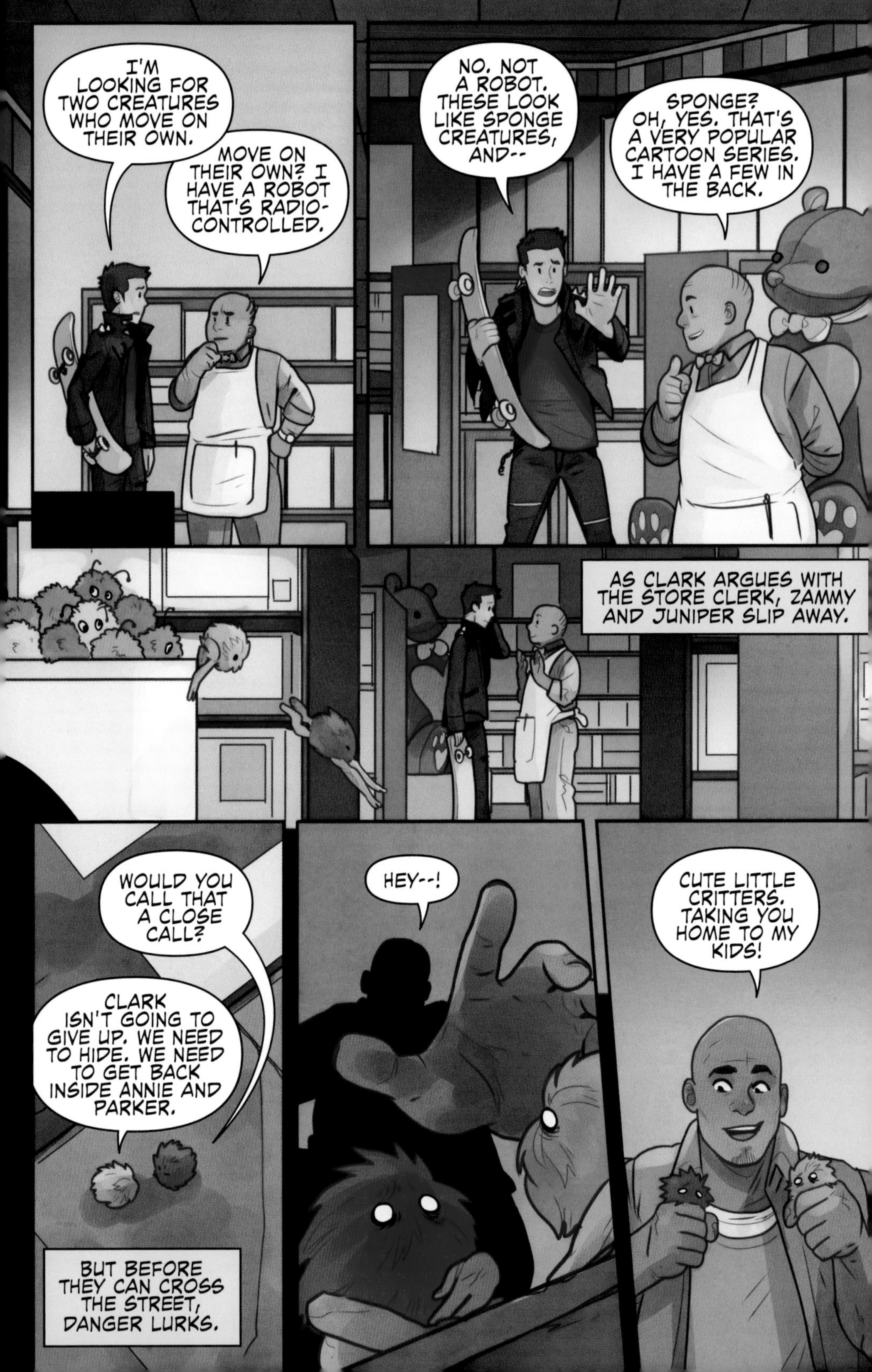
I'M LOOKING FOR TWO CREATURES WHO MOVE ON THEIR OWN.
MOVE ON THEIR OWN? I HAVE A ROBOT THAT'S RADIO-CONTROLLED.
NO. NOT A ROBOT. THESE LOOK LIKE SPONGE CREATURES, AND--
SPONGE? OH, YES. THAT'S A VERY POPULAR CARTOON SERIES. I HAVE A FEW IN THE BACK.
AS CLARK ARGUES WITH THE STORE CLERK, ZAMMY AND JUNIPER SLIP AWAY.
WOULD YOU CALL THAT A CLOSE CALL?
CLARK ISN'T GOING TO GIVE UP. WE NEED TO HIDE. WE NEED TO GET BACK INSIDE ANNIE AND PARKER.
BUT BEFORE THEY CAN CROSS THE STREET, DANGER LURKS.
HEY--!
CUTE LITTLE CRITTERS. TAKING YOU HOME TO MY KIDS!